CW01207252

"Tabbie's original and unusual plots and really intriguing read."

Dave Andrews, Presenter, *BBC Radio Leicester*

"The master of supernatural suspense."

Peter J Bennett, *Author*

"The books are catching, they keep you thinking, and make you 'look outside the box'. I enjoy reading Tabbie's books in my limited down time."

Anne Royle and Spook (my four legged glasses).
Founder *Pathfinder Guide Dog Programme*

"Tabbie's skilful tale weaving grips, shocks and inspires every time and leaves you feeling that these narratives are coming with a deeper message from the world of Spirit. I always look forward to each new novel that she has crafted, with great anticipation."

Karen, *Indigo Aura Spiritual*

The Hole Will Get You

Other Books by this Author

THE JENNY TRILOGY
White Noise is Heavenly Blue
The Spiral
Choler

A Fair Collection
The Unforgivable Error
No-Don't!
Above The Call
A Bit Of Fresh
A Bit Of Spare
The Paws Of Spiritual Justice
Sever His Member

NOTICE

Please note that the author's website
www.tabbiebrowneauthor.com
has now been closed.
For information on all books,
please visit Amazon where they are available
in paperback and also on Kindle.
Also check her Author Central page.
You can also buy paperbacks direct from Lulu Publishing.

The Hole Will Get You

Tabbie Browne

Copyright © 2019 Tabbie Browne

All rights reserved, including the right to reproduce this book, or portions thereof in any form. No part of this text may be reproduced, transmitted, downloaded, decompiled, reverse engineered, or stored, in any form or introduced into any information storage and retrieval system, in any form or by any means, whether electronic or mechanical without the express written permission of the author.

This is a work of fiction. Names and characters are the product of the author's imagination and any resemblance to actual persons, living or dead, is entirely coincidental.

The views expressed in this work are solely those of the author and do not necessarily reflect the views of the publisher, and the publisher hereby disclaims any responsibility for them.

ISBN: 978-0-244-21046-5

PublishNation
www.publishnation.co.uk

This book is dedicated to one of our readers:

ALISON

now at rest.
A lovely person with a beautiful heart.

Foreword

This will be different to anything you have read
and your thoughts will have to be focused.

You are extremely privileged to be allowed this insight.

Do not ask the author to explain any of it
for she is merely the tool for our communication
and she doesn't have to understand the words
that are sent through her.

Open your mind and realise that all you see and all you hear
may not be as you previously took for granted.

Welcome to the very edge of this strange world
but if you find it hard to believe, don't shoot the messenger!

One thing is for sure.
You will never look at Mars in the same way again.

Can you accept the challenge?

Chapter 1

"You watching that crap again? It's all a load of—"

Before Kieran could come out with his usual profanity his sister cut in.

"It wouldn't hurt you to use your brain for once instead of watching a load of men kicking a ball around."

He stormed out of the room and stamped all the way upstairs knowing it would annoy her.

Sue was stretched out on the sofa watching a recording she'd made of an astronomy programme. Even as a small child she had found the whole subject fascinating and when asked what she wanted for birthdays and Christmas the answer was always the same. Books on the moon, the planets and now the universe.

She hadn't long left college and had managed to get a job at a local shopping mall which wasn't going to be a career but brought in some money for now. She had applied to various universities in the hopes of going into research and achieving her dream of working on a space programme. For now it was a case of waiting and hoping.

Her brother being only sixteen was still at a local academy and although his dream was to become a famous footballer, there was little chance of it actually coming to fruition. His parents considered it wasn't a proper job and he should set his sights on something practical.

Just as Sue was getting engrossed again in her programme, the door burst open and Kieran almost demanded what was for dinner because he was starving. She sighed as she hit the pause button.

"I've done a cottage pie. It's in the oven." She glanced at her watch.

"I'm starving. Are there any biscuits? And why's mum so late?"

She sat up.

"Firstly no, you aren't starving, people in the third world are starving. What's stopping you looking in the biscuit tin? And if you use that excuse for a brain, you will remember mum has had to pop over to Gran's on the way home from work, she's having her operation soon and she's worried about it."

Ignoring the reply he said "Well why can't I have mine?"

How long this would have gone on was anyone's guess, for at that moment the front door opened and Denise came in looking very tired.

"Hi Mum." Sue was on her feet and went to greet her. "You look as though you could do with a cuppa."

"Oh. Those buses. I had to stand and he kept braking."

Sue took her coat while she sat down.

"I'm glad you're here, she won't give me my dinner." Kieran was hovering.

Denise looked up at him.

"Don't start please. I've had enough today."

The look his sister gave him could have knocked him over.

"I'm going to get mum a drink then I'll dish up." She hissed. Then to her mum "Should I leave some for Dad?"

"Yes please, he can put it in the microwave when he gets in."

Although the parents Denise and John were approaching middle age she was looking much older than her years. They had been in the same class at school and been in a relationship since then but when they were both twenty, Denise got pregnant and they decided to get married straight away. So at only thirty nine she had raised two children, was working, had a husband on shifts and was looking out for her widowed mother who, in her mid sixties was still very active physically but worried about every little thing as though it was a major incident.

"Have you got course work to do young man?" She called after her son as he dumped his plate in the kitchen and was heading for the stairs to go to his room.

"Yep." Was all she got in return.

There was no point in telling him to get on with it. If he did, he did, she was too weary just now to enforce it.

The guardians covering the family worked in harmony with each other. If one had a problem the others made sure the unsettling ripples were quelled. Although no names are needed in the spirit world, for purpose of identification the guardians of this family are tagged with a name beginning with the same letter or sound as their charge.

Kieran's angel Kane was the one with the most demands on his expertise but, while maintaining the harmony, he was equally aware that this was a young man approaching adulthood and he couldn't let him be confined to the extent that his own character couldn't develop. He was going through the 'know it all' phase but that would fade and hopefully a fine upright person would emerge. Sometimes the other angels didn't agree with him but he knew what he was doing and had to stand his ground.

He now hovered over the lad who was studying his football magazines. His text books were on the bed at the side of him but he had little intention of giving them much thought for now. He'd do it later.

Kane put himself in a position over him and projected the thought.

"I'll do it now."

Kieran visibly shuddered. The magazine fell from his left hand while his right one reached for the history book. He sat bolt upright. What was going on? He pushed the book away and waited. Again his hand reached for it but when he tried to retract it, he couldn't. It was as though he was stuck to it. The bravado had gone. In desperation he decided to go with the force and held the text book in both hands. This time there was no interference. He turned the pages until he came to the piece he had to study. All was calm in the room.

At this point it must be explained that not all is as it seems. You have a picture before you of a pretty normal family and you believe it as would anyone else, not only in the physical world, but also any passing evil spirit on the look out for any situation that needed mischievously stirring up, or by good spirits who were glad to see that all appeared fairly calm.

For this is one of the cleverest charades only played out by top notch entities for whatever purpose, usually only known to them.

They can be after a particular target, or doing a general reconnoitre of an area after reports of something unsavoury going on. It can take a while to execute and can only stay in operation for a certain time so that they are not detected. But keep in mind that time, space and distance in the spiritual world is far different from our earthly understanding. A couple of decades in the mortal existence could be the blink of an eye in another dimension, so we have to observe this from our concept but never forget we are spanning different comparisons. You wouldn't tell someone in New York that because it is five o'clock in England it had to be five o'clock there. That is a start of how you must think.

Now to get back to our normal family. This placing had to be planned from the start, so Denise and John had to be born within a short space of time, go to the same school, get married and have the children fairly quickly. It was no accident that they had to get married, as it was all part of the plan. When Kieran arrived the group was complete.

Again, a short explanation is needed because this is something a bit different.

It is common knowledge that we have at least one guardian angel to watch over us. In this case Denise has Dee, John has Jay, Sue has Essie and Kieran is watched by Kane. But there is a reason for the connection in names and it only applies to these four, no one else in the family.

The guardian angels and their charges are not two separate entities. They are one. So Denise and Dee are one spirit giving the appearance of two so that evil onlookers have no idea of the high level angels watching them. In body they have to give a believable performance, hence Kieran's attitude, Sue's caring, Denise looking a bit weary. In body they would feel these things but their spirit side would be on permanent alert and observing every minute detail. Also, if they thought they were being watched, a stand in guardian would hover in full view over one of their bodies while their own guardian side went off to follow up someone or something. The stand ins were just as high up the ladder but were not in body at the moment, and the four currently in situ had done the same when they were solely in spirit.

So why were these four planted in a certain place? The semi detached they owned was lost among dozens more in the area on the outskirts of a busy town. It didn't stand out for obvious reasons and again it was a case of being hidden in plain sight. But the reason for this particular venue held a sinister objective. Something evil was already well settled, not only here but near other towns. No cities or little villages had been chosen, just reasonably sized market towns which were quite busy and large enough that the residents didn't know everyone. So people could come and go without too much question.

To date the reason behind it all was a mystery. But more importantly, they had to learn who was being targeted. All they knew was that a watcher had noticed a pattern of evil vibes emitting from these areas which could have been just an amateur attempt at a bit of black magic for fun. If so that could soon be squashed and would have been dealt with by lesser spirits, but this had the feel of something more sinister. Also the question arose as to whether it was a possible attack on the living or the spirits in that area. But they were soon to get their first major lead.

The 'watchers' from the good angels were noticing a build up of evil concentration. When there is any quantity of good or bad it creates a change in the surrounding air. For example if a group of good people congregated and send healing vibes in what ever form to someone in need, the space around them would, to put it in simple terms, glow. And the more effort that went in, the larger the glow.

But what the watchers were finding was anything but, in fact it was a building evil presence that was making its roots, possibly as a central control which would then spread out to other small towns in the area and possibly taking in any villages in its path. Although it wouldn't centre on a village, it certainly wouldn't ignore any easy pickings.

This didn't seem to be a large presence at the moment and what interested the watchers was that usually these would have grown by now. This one seemed quite small in size but it was the intensity of the evil that bothered them. It would seem to be resting one minute then the next it would flare up and be pulsing. Then after a while it would abate.

An idea ran through the hierarchy of good angels. A scan would be done, firstly of the nearby area, then spreading out further afield. They needed to find out if there was any remote connection between the surges and any occurrence elsewhere. If so, the local cell was controlling the action from afar without having to go near their targets. This would make them very difficult to trace and there would be no lead back to their base. But all this may change so a task force was immediately deployed to try and find a pattern. These would have to be very high angels as any low ones would be detected immediately and the plan would have to be scrapped. The two leaders took on the identity of Wren and Finch and sent out a handful of very experienced spirits to do the initial ground work.

Their one concern was that the source appeared to be coming from a suburb of a market town. The area was fairly quiet and it was a respectable neighbourhood with no trouble, drug dealing or anything to disturb the everyday run of things. Adults went to work, children went to school, people walked their dogs, mowed their front lawns and generally had nothing to worry about. And this was the area where Denise and her family lived.

It had already been observed that all the guardians in the area were diligently protecting the ones in their care and normally they would have been alerted to be extra watchful, but in severe cases secrecy was important as any communication could be detected by whatever this evil was. No one on any level must know they were even taking an interest.

It was Sunday morning and although half way through June, the weather wasn't as warm as one would have expected. Denise went outside to get a 'feel of it' as she put it and shuddered so went back in quickly. Everyone else was in still in bed and she mentally ran through what she had to do that day. Although nobody else was in favour she would get John to fetch her mum round for dinner. There wouldn't be much conversation, the two teenagers would have their heads buried in their phones most of the time so conversation would be limited to her and John if he felt like it. But she had made the rule that there were no phones allowed at the table. This didn't go down very well with all sorts of protests.

“But Mum, Rosie is ringing and I’ve just got to know what happened.”

Despite the pouts that didn’t wash.

Kieran’s main excuse was usually that he had to be in continual contact because, and then followed the first thing he could think of at the time.

Denise was so used to it that she let it wash over her.

But when her phone was put on the side table in case Gran rang the children felt that was double standards. At least John did support her on that by reminding them that Gran could be in urgent need of help whereas the fact that one of their mates had got pregnant or got someone else pregnant was not a reason to let food go cold.

As the good watchers observed the household in passing, all seemed normal except for one thing. A report went straight back to Finch to observe from afar, so that no evil could pick up on the observation.

Wren and Finch and others on their level and above, had their own ways of observing without being detected but that is not for lesser spirits to know. So, on receiving the instant message, Finch immediately homed in on the street where the family lived and sure enough there was a trace which seemed to evaporate immediately. This was cause for concern as it could mean the angel attention had been spotted and that could only have happened if the evil was of the same or higher standing. That posed the question as to why something that high needed to have made a base or even a sub station here.

Immediately Wren and Finch were in communication as to the best tactic. They could hold off as though nothing had been detected but they needed to be aware of what was festering, because something obviously was going on. These two not only sat at the head of the operation but had an extra power. They could downsize, that is they could throw off their high rank and become a simple spirit going about its business, even appearing a bit simple at times which was a perfect trap. So it was decided that as Finch had already surveyed the scene, Wren would be the best choice so there could be no connection.

As Denise was preparing for the day, little did she realise what was about to go on around them. Her alter ego as her own guardian was nothing more than a protector and she was too concerned with making Sunday run as smooth as possible to worry about anything else and her mind turned to what vegetables to have for dinner.

Chapter 2

As in a place of work there are many departments with each having its own specialist team, the same applies to all aspects of existence in whatever form, especially the spiritual. On earth we are aware of the police, probationary services, courts, prisons, etc who deal with offenders against the person or peace. In spirit it goes a lot further than that. On earth we are familiar with someone's life being terminated as the ultimate punishment, whether everyone agrees or not. The priest will pray for the soul but then what? In the spirit world there is an even more final punishment.

But this information will be fed in small doses as it would be too much to comprehend all at once. Let us just say for now that it doesn't necessarily apply to anything done in your earth time.

Hope, the angel guardian of Hannah, Denise's mum was separate, so unlike the rest there were two spirits in presence. Gran, as Hannah was known wasn't really that old but to the youngsters she seemed ancient and not with it at all. At sixty six she had retired and did voluntary work to give herself some purpose in life, but to hear the young ones talk, she was long past it. At the local hospital she served at the little shop, made tea and enjoyed meeting all the different people.

If you asked Kieran what she did, he wouldn't have a clue and probably think she sat on her backside all day staring at the wall. Sue was kind to her but still didn't take much interest in how she spent her days. She was there, and they'd miss her when she was gone but that was about it. John just went with the flow, would give her a lift now and again according to what shift he was on but mainly did what Denise asked him to like putting up a shelf or things she couldn't manage.

Denise was the dutiful daughter and sometimes seemed to overdo the concern but at least she bothered so they all let her get on with it. Now she went to the phone to check mum was alright.

"Hello Mum. You ok?"

"Yes thank you. How are you?"

This was the normal start to the conversation.

"John will be getting you about twelve as usual Mum. You will be ready won't you?"

Hannah sighed. "I'm not a geriatric you know. I can get myself ready."

"I know Mum, just saying."

They said their goodbyes each having a mutter to themselves.

Denise thought her mum should be grateful because a lot of elderly people had nobody, whereas Hannah wished she wouldn't be so patronising and treat her like an imbecile. But she wouldn't say anything as at least the girl bothered.

Wren had a certain way of working. Whenever he observed one person, family or group, he always did what he called his 'offshoot'. That meant that he followed the line out to anyone connected with anyone he was observing. He'd done an initial scan on the teenagers and their friends and before he checked out Denise and John he decided to give Hannah the once over.

The thing that hit him immediately was that she had a separate guardian, whereas the other four were self equipped as he called it. Knowing he mustn't be too conspicuous if they were on a special placing mission he thought he would see if he could find anything out from the gran. Although it only took him a millisecond, there was nothing to give him any clue and she obviously wasn't connected with it. So he would have to watch the others from afar and by devious means.

He and Finch were always curious when a covert operation was in place and one thing Wren liked to do was check them out in case anything could be useful in the future.

The most obvious answer was that they were there to sift out the evil that was hanging around and he could sense its presence quite strongly.

These little teams that put themselves on the front line took a lot of risks, not only from being discovered, but from the wrath of whatever evil they were confronting. They were always very experienced and had a few battle scars to prove it. Wren didn't stay long in the area so that his presence would only seem to be passing through. But he had already been noticed, so what they were dealing with was something very experienced and probably high level.

Finch observing from afar immediately picked up on this and did a sweep to erase any trace of Wren's wake, the trail left by a spirit. The evil would be aware they had been noticed but at that stage not by whom. But that was no consolation for they would know it was a high power and every further observation would be monitored. So from the good side, they would have to be watched by other means.

Time for a little more insight. The spiritual section from which Wren and Finch operate is totally confined to catching evil on the run who are trying to escape total wipeout. Think of it in human terms. If a criminal has been given the death sentence but escaped, they wouldn't wait around to be caught, and due to the chemical make up of their brain, they would have no compassion to anyone who posed a threat. They would destroy anything in their path to avoid the death penalty because to them that would be the end of life as they like it, regardless of any afterlife.

Now think of this in terms of the spirit world. It isn't just a beautiful place filled with love and peace, the evil pass on as well. Hence the eternal fight. So even if you have got away with the most heinous crimes on earth, that is merely the beginning and justice will be done by the heavenly executioners. This is not a pleasant job but as they say, somebody's got to do it.

Although the special groups work under cover, the very high levels usually have some idea of where they are and who they are targeting. In this case the Denise family set up couldn't be traced to any particular section. It wasn't unknown, for secrecy had to be the key for it to be successful. But it always triggered interest and sometimes the hierarchy felt a little peeved at not being trusted with the knowledge.

But one member of Finch's team had an idea which related to a previous experience which they now shared with the group.

"It goes back many years, even centuries. Someone did some of the most disgusting things imaginable to a young girl resulting in her death. She was barely recognisable. The family were so distraught they vowed never to rest until the perpetrator had been brought to justice. Of course they all died eventually and everyone thought that was the end of it.

But every so many years since, another family seems to appear, identical to the original one and they seem to be searching out the murderer. We think they must wait for them to be reborn then come back themselves to do justice on earth. Every time they hook onto an innocent soul who has no connection whatsoever with either side, possibly to give them credence."

There was a pause while the group mulled it over then Wren summed it up.

"So they are here to find the murderer, who must also be in body, and they can't be far away or the family wouldn't have chosen this location."

Another member added "But we have to be careful how we watch or they will pick up on us in an instant."

Wren was still a bit concerned.

"So do we think they are only out for physical justice, just to satisfy themselves?"

"Seems that way." Finch thought. "They don't seem high enough for 'total'.

"That can't be done from the physical anyway." Another added.

There was another pause and everyone was thinking the same but Finch voiced it.

"Unless they are being used. Yes of course they want revenge as a family but think about it. We thought they must be quite high up the ladder, as they aren't easy to detect, but are they actually controlling it themselves, or has another force jumped on board and cloaked them so they can execute their own plan under cover?"

"You mean we are concentrating on the family but it's what's behind them that we should really be detecting." Wren said.

Again there was silence while this was mulled over.

One of the team then asked "Is Hannah in danger?"

“Don’t think so.” Finch decided. “She’s too good a cover and has no idea of anything so probably safe but I think we should be ready in case she needs help.”

“You know, if all this is true, I don’t think it would hurt to have the odd look at the family now and again. Anything that is holding them may think that’s all we are watching. They wouldn’t know we had any idea of what’s really going on” One of the members suggested.

“That’s true.” Another agreed. “If we suddenly pulled back, wouldn’t that look as though we were onto them?”

Finch stepped in here.

“You both have good points. But for now I think we will only do a distance scan until we know more. Don’t forget, a lot of this is only supposition, we don’t have the proof yet.”

“But I think we have to exercise caution until we are sure.” Wren added.

The meeting was over but a new slant had been put on the situation and they would all be happier when they were certain of what was really going on, whatever the outcome.

Dinner was finished and Kieran had disappeared up to his room as usual. Sue was helping her mum wash up and John was nodding off in the chair.

“I hope you’re not going to snore.” Hannah tutted.

A grunt was all she got in reply.

As Denise and Sue came back into the room she said “I’ve told him I hope he doesn’t snore.”

“Well he does work shifts mum and his body clock’s all over the place.”

“I’m off then Mum, ok?” Sue went off to her room to get ready to go round to her friend’s house.

“Will you be back for tea?” Denise called after her.

“No ta. We’re going for a burger.”

There was a snort from Hannah.

“They don’t know what proper food is these days do they?”

“What you talking about?” Denise was tired and didn’t need any such comments.

“They fill themselves with junk then wonder why they get spots.”

There was an audible sigh.

"We have burgers sometimes. Anyway, she's a good girl and she's got a nice friend."

There was definitely something in the tone that said 'and that's an end to it'.

"Do you want the telly on Mam?"

There was no reply. Hannah was fast asleep.

The evil had certainly noticed the good angels' presence but it didn't concern them too much. As they had left it could mean that they didn't think it worth the monitoring, or they could be awaiting the next move. But this evil felt it could take on anything and as soon as it achieved the job it was there to do, it would be gone.

This may be a good time to explain some of the remarks made by the spirits and take you further into an unknown sphere, if you feel you can cope with it.

On earth everyone is familiar with execution in whatever form, hanging, lethal injection etc. It is the ultimate penalty. Losing your life is the worst thing that can happen. We are not talking about natural death but one that is imposed as a punishment for wrongdoings.

In the spirit world you have probably heard that all your sins are forgiven and you will know eternal peace. On one side that may be true, but we are looking at the other side for everything is not all rosy and happy as some would have you believe. And there are special spirits who have the unsavoury job of terminating those who are so evil they are beyond redemption. Of course the decision isn't taken lightly and may have spanned centuries of earth time, but in very extreme cases, they have to be erased permanently.

Black holes are now widely studied and even photographed with modern technology, but again this is physical. Imagine it in the spirit world. Stop for a moment and just think what that means. Here is a very simple explanation although what you are about to be privy to learn is anything but and only known in detail to a very select few.

To 'total' a spirit is to condemn them to a magenta hole. They are escorted to the event horizon, which is a tricky operation because, as with black holes there is no obvious line you must not cross. The executioner spirits then propel the subject at such a speed they cannot retaliate and are sucked in and stretched until they are obliterated forever. Total annihilation.

This means that if the good angels were observing such an entity with that end in mind, it must be guilty of intense evil. And it may not be working alone. Therefore such possible groups such as those in the area of the family may be part of or even the entire force which was here for revenge. But with the good angels experience they knew that this may have nothing to do with such an operation. A lot of these incidents were red herrings for a bigger target, or just junior spirits seeking revenge of their own.

A quick observation of Denise's family didn't show any real intensity but something could be just attaching itself to make a temporary base until they were ready to move on.

But the question was, why were they acting as their own guardians? This wasn't an everyday thing so they were either good watchers for the events in that area, or they were the evil itself. Either way, Wren and Finch couldn't just dive in and ask if they were friend or foe! For now they had to play the familiar waiting game and keep their thoughts open for any eventuality.

Chapter 3

Hannah woke with a start. "Get away from me!" She yelled then opened her eyes and stared at John.

"Mam, what's the matter?" Denise was at her side.

"I –I – don't know. Oh I'm here aren't I?"

"You've been dreaming Mam, its ok now. You're safe."

Hannah looked from Denise to John who had woken up himself now.

"What's up?" He yawned.

"It's ok, Mam's had a bad dream."

He grunted. "Was I in it?"

He meant it as a joke but her expression surprised him.

"Yes but I didn't like it. You had a knife and…"

"Did I use it?" He was playing with her and a smirk crept over his face.

"No."

"Well, that's alright then isn't it?"

His levity didn't go down very well and Denise sensed a tightness in the air so she said she'd go and make them all a cup of tea. Her mother was casting suspicious glances at John which could have been amusing to watch but he ignored it thinking she was having a senior moment.

Hope was in close contact to soothe her but she too had been aware of something in the area which was very unpleasant. It had no sooner come than it had left with no trace. She strengthened the protection around Hannah and soothed her inwardly until the dream faded.

As mentioned, a common practice among guardians in cases where evil could be hovering is to hire another angel of the same level to 'sit' for a while so that the guard can leave to communicate with higher levels and not attract any interest from evil watchers.

This isn't confined to times when there is possible danger or it would be too obvious and sometimes the angels will dart around from one to another just to create confusion.

On this occasion it was a genuine call, for Hope remembered something that had happened years before and she needed to check it out straight away. Wren was waiting for her because he too had recalled the incident. In a previous life Hannah had been plagued by a mischievous spirit while she was in her teens. Nothing unusual there as it is quite common for youngsters in puberty to experience strange spiritual happenings.

But this one was a bit different. It became so real, she actually believed there was someone else there that only she could see. It was a girl who said she was her twin sister but had died at birth and she needed her to know she was there and accept her. Her parents strongly denied this and had taken her to the local priest for help but the spirit would leave at such times so there was nothing to find or exorcise. So the poor girl lived the rest of that earth life with the spirit at her side. Hope of course had witnessed all of this but the strange thing was that the girl spirit didn't have a guardian of her own. In the case of twins there is usually one guard for each child and sometimes a third one overseeing.

Finch had joined the meeting.

"Has Hannah had this situation in other lives?" He wondered.

"No," Wren had already checked that. "And in this life she is an only one."

"So has the previous supposed twin come back now?" Hope asked.

"I doubt that." Finch was quick to say. "Whatever is starting to bother her now isn't there for her health. We've traced a faint wake and it isn't a good one."

"But why her? I've kept a very close watch on her constantly. She's no threat to anyone is she?" Hope wanted to know.

Wren had to state the obvious.

"How can we ever be sure? Some of these other spirits are masters of disguise. Maybe one feels it has a score to settle."

It was decided that Hope would stay in full view carrying out her normal protection but there would be a higher back up for a while who would notice any interest from other parties. She was advised to put any of these thoughts from her so as not to give any clue that an alert had been raised.

On returning to the house Hope acknowledged the stand in and resumed her position just behind Hannah who now seemed to have forgotten the dream. The 'baby sitter' had done a good job of wiping any unpleasant feeling from her.

But one thing was rather obvious. Jay, John's alter spirit seemed to be scrutinising her as she chatted to Denise. Trying not to appear interested, Hope floated around a bit trying to pick up the vibes in the room. There was a distinct feeling of unrest but where was it? One minute it was over John but then it was in front of Hannah as though it was trying to block her from Denise. Also she felt she was being pushed away so that she had no control to protect Hannah. She was now in a very vulnerable position for strictly speaking she was the only free guardian in the house as the others posing as them were the same entity. There was no good trying to hide the fact she knew this for the atmosphere was electric and everyone apart from Hannah knew the score.

This bothered Wren and Finch for the situation had suddenly taken a turn, and not for the better.

Kieran appeared to be asleep on his bed, but Kane was nowhere in the room. When spirits split in this way it gives the appearance to the uneducated that they are in one place, that is where the body is but the soul is free to wander often under another guise so that it isn't recognised.

It was suggested that it is just the same when we are asleep but then the soul is tied by its light line to its physical form so there is always a connection. If that gets broken the person dies. But in this case the four in this family can split completely then return when they wish. It is this particular skill that identifies them as higher spirits, but which? Both good and evil have this power and although some lower levels are aware of it, some find it hard to understand.

Kane had actually taken his father's place. John as Jay had been scouting round a certain area but as soon as he woke up, Kane took over. Finch realised they were both targeting the same place and knew they must watch to see if the two females did the same. Wren had a strong feeling now that these were not on the good side so all of them must be watched but covertly so he sent a secret message to his higher levels requesting observation be done by highly skilled angels who were expert in not being traced. How they did it was known only to them and not even Wren and Finch would be aware of the methods used. But something was brewing and had to be detected before it was too late.

If Denise in her physical form thought it was nice that her daughter had good friend of her own age, as Dee she had another opinion. Lisa was anything but the innocent eighteen year old she portrayed. She liked to give the appearance of not understanding jokes and giving a far away look when she didn't want to answer any probing questions. But it wasn't the physical side that bothered her, it was the spiritual, for this girl was anything but a novice in any field. In previous lives she had never been short of men and when she had been born into a male body she bedded as many females as it was physically possible to do.

It was obvious that a sexually motivated spirit was reappearing as this female to carry on where it left off and it wasn't necessarily on the low scale. Its trick was to dispense with any guardian allocated and bring in its own. After a while the good angels would manage to remove the evil guardian and replace it. Then it would all be repeated. This in itself proved that it was pretty clever as usually an angel stays with a subject though all its earth lives.

So if this one was from a higher plane why did it only concentrate on the sexual side? It didn't seem to lust for murder or anything aggressive, just gratification. But that meant it wasn't going anywhere or moving on, just staying where it was. It didn't make sense, so it had to be a smoke screen.

Wren suggested it was to keep watchers occupied in the hope they would give up as a useless task, then it would go for its real target. Finch agreed but added that it was possible that this was the evil they sensed in connection with the family. By befriending Sue, it was free to be in contact at any time.

They did a spirit rewind to see if that's what had frightened Hannah and although something had definitely been involved it wasn't Lisa's guardian.

One thing was certain. It wasn't just one evil entity at work in the area, there could even be several, all on separate missions and that could lead to territory wars as boundaries were trespassed.

The girls were stretched out on Lisa's bed. They'd been experimenting with nail polish, make up and all the things that age group do.

"So did you get that job I told you about?" Sue was examining her nails.

"Nah. Went for it but they're all a load of bellends. Couldn't work there."

"Well I've no intention of stopping there but it brings in some cash." Sue was a bit peeved. She did all she could to try and get her friend into some sort of employment but it was as though she just wanted to sail through life without a care as long as she had somewhere to live and the freedom to come and go as she liked.

"You've got to do something." She insisted turning to look at her. "Nobody can go on like you are. What's your mam say?"

"Do you know," Lisa sat up and turned on Sue "you sound a lot like her."

"What?"

"You're becoming a drag on me. You never want to go out and hang around, you don't want to do this, you don't want to do that. You're becoming boring."

Sue sat up now appearing rather hurt.

"How can you even think that? I do all I can to help you but you just shove it back in my face. Hey what's that?" She'd noticed a large bruise on the back of Lisa's shoulder.

"That? Oh it's nothing. Always banging on something."

While they carried on with this banter, Lisa's current guardian was studying Sue aka Essie. She had come across this single soul factor a few times and always been told to ignore it for the same reasons as the higher levels did but the thought flitted past that this one could be monitoring Lisa. At the first opportunity she would report it to a higher level as she wasn't sure if it was good or bad as the vibes weren't clear so that in itself was strange.

But the guardian didn't get the chance, for no sooner had the thought vanished that Lisa had her replaced and she was gone.

The word spread instantly and Finch mentally descended to the disposed angel's level for an exact account, after which she was moved to another area. On returning Wren told him that Lisa could be an innocent player in this and was trying to carry on with her usual lustful habits but was being controlled by a stronger force who were grooming her for much more sinister purposes.

"So that in itself could cause a conflict." Wren thought. "She won't want to be led off in any other direction, unless sex is involved of course."

"That could be it!" Finch knew he'd hit on something. "That's how they will draw her, with bait. It will only be when she's in their grasp that she'll realise she's been set up and then wait for the explosion."

Wren agreed. "Because, as we know, she's not from a low level but always seems to have worked alone. She won't accept being ruled."

"Or he." Finch corrected. "Just depends on which gender he or she is using currently."

"Well we know, it's Lisa."

"Don't be too sure."

"Eh?" Wren had an idea where this was leading but surely it would stay with its current one for this earth life.

There was silence for a moment then Finch voiced what they both realised. This entity could be what it wanted, male, female, both or even possibly animal. Now there was pause for thought.

Denise was watching the clock. She was very restricted while Hannah was there and had things to do, but not about the house. As soon as they had finished tea she would get John to run her Mum home armed with a few pieces of cake etc.

Anyone casually observing this family would think they were as normal as it was possible to be, but that was their skill and how it was supposed to appear.

Jay was mentally in touch with Kane but the place they were watching wasn't forthcoming so decided to move their attentions elsewhere and Kane re-entered Kieran for now until they decided on the next move.

Sue decided to go home early. She hadn't enjoyed this visit and felt her friend was tired of her and would probably ditch her soon. But as Essie, that was what she wanted to portray and knew she must keep some sort of contact, so would ring her the following day. She would play the 'I'm sorry' bit and 'we're still friends aren't we' so that Lisa would feel superior. She knew this person always had to be better than anyone else and treated anyone she felt she could control like dirt. Essie hated it and despised her for it but that was the only way she could stay on board so for now that was how it would have to be. If she showed any sign of exerting herself, she would be out.

So now, a little while later the family were all at home sitting quietly together but only the highly trained could be even remotely aware of the communication being exchanged between them for it was over in a millisecond but they all knew their next moves.

"It may be nothing but I'll have it checked."

Finch had noticed a sudden increase in negativity in the next little town. Things were going wrong for people, not big things but a run of incidents that were upsetting the smooth running of life causing unrest. Wren had also been watching another one in the opposite direction where there had been a sudden upsurge in deaths. Not elderly people but mostly middle aged fairly healthy folk who were suddenly terminated. It didn't make sense. He quickly studied the death reports and found that these had no previous medical history of anything life threatening but suddenly they had suffered fatal heart attacks. Even the local police became suspicious but their enquiries led nowhere. This made the angels look at the whole area and what they found came as a big surprise. Each of the small towns around the one where the family lived seemed to be going through a similar phase but each one for a different reason. One was experienced a lot of theft from houses, cars etc, while in anothers people were complaining of acute skin problems.

"I know what this is. Seen it before." Finch was onto it but so was Wren.

"Distraction."

"Exactly. While everyone is running around with what seems to be a major problem, no-one's attention is on what is really going on."

But Wren stated another obvious fact which didn't make sense if these were highly trained evil forces.

"So why leave this town untouched? It only draws more attention to it."

After a moment's thought they both knew the answer. That's exactly what was being planned. The upset and inconvenience in other towns meant nothing to the plotters as they had no conscience or compassion and it didn't matter who got hurt as long as they achieved their objective. The target had to be in the family's town. But if they were behind it, why bring it to their doorstep. It was usual to operate from afar and hide your identity. On the other hand if they were not responsible, it meant that another force was after them and they were in the firing line.

It was time for extra vigilance and highly skilled watchers would have to be brought in. These didn't have to stay undercover for they were so clever they could walk right through the middle of a problem and never be suspected. Again, the secret of how they worked was for them to know. No questions were asked but they were referred to as Merge. They never had to be summoned but just infiltrated into a situation. It may be suspected that they were in situ but no-one, either in physical or purely spiritual state would know who they were. They didn't suddenly appear but would ride tandem on any available host and merge, hence the nickname, with any guardian they chose. Then jump to another and another, even to living things like trees, insects or whatever they found suitable to fit in with the current problem. They would also lead false trails, but that was only a fraction of the skill, the rest is unknown and has to remain so.

"They are probably already there." Wren mused.

"Undoubtedly," Finch agreed "which means it is on the upper scale."

This immediately put it into the category of presenting acute danger, not only to targets but anything connected with them.

Hannah had settled down for the night and as soon as she was drifting off to sleep she was aware of Hope who had been making her sleepy so that she could communicate with her. This didn't surprise the mother as it happened on a regular basis and she was fully aware of her presence, but it was all wiped when she awoke and any snippet she did recall she put down to a dream.

"So what was John up to?" Hope got straight to the point.

Hannah had to think for a minute as the experience had been dimmed during her waking time, but slowly Hope let it emerge.

"I don't know, in fact I'm not even sure that it was him, just someone who looked a bit like him." She was trying to recall what had happened.

"Was he menacing?"

"It was strange, I was held by something but he didn't seem to be touching me then…." She trailed off as though not sure.

Hope let her think for a moment then prompted.

"Was he holding something?"

"Oh yes, a knife and I thought he was going to kill me."

There was a pause before Hope continued.

"You see, I was there and something else was, but it didn't appear to be John. You're sure it was him?"

"I'm not sure now, I just thought it was at the time."

Hope placed herself right next to Hannah.

"Think carefully and this may sound strange. Could it have been a female?"

"What?"

"Are you sure it was a man, whether it was John or not?"

Hannah was becoming agitated.

"No, I'm sure it wasn't a woman. But I got the impression it was a man and I thought it was John."

"Alright, that's enough for now, you've been very helpful."

"But I haven't told you anything."

Hope soothed the vibes around her and sent her off to a calm sleep, keeping a careful watch over her. It seemed obvious that the 'twin' hadn't been in presence this time, but something had and she didn't know what. The information had gone to Wren in a mini blink.

Denise and John were in bed. They carried on a normal conversation about the children, her mother and other day to day occurrences so that any onlooker would have no idea about their sole presence, apart from astute ones that could spot the single spirit, but they had a habit of splitting the two images so an uneducated passing spirit would think, say for example, Denise had Dee watching but not notice it was a duplicate.

As they said 'Goodnight' and settled down, they were unaware that they were not alone in the room. Something was hovering over them. It stayed for a few seconds then had gone but the speed had disturbed the air and both sat bolt upright.

"Did you feel that?" John whispered.

"Yes. What do you think it was?"

"Don't know but we'd better put up extra protection. Something was definitely here, and it wasn't friendly."

They communicated with Sue and Kieran and warned them to shield themselves in case of a return visit.

All this had been noted by distance watchers and they knew only too well that the visitor was not there as a friend but was scanning the place.

So the possibility was that maybe the local activity was building round them but they were the sitting ducks in the middle of the pond. But who could be after them?

Chapter 4

Although the details were not known, some very high powers sensed when there was going to be another magenta hole total extinction. Only certain very strong spirits were chosen as the officers, for the evil was so strong that it could fake its demeanour in a last bid for freedom or use every bit of strength it could summon to escape the ultimate end. The numbers of attendants had been increased gradually as the evil got stronger and whereas long ago it only took one executioner, the present four had been increased to six but with others standing by in case they were needed for a particularly nasty one.

The six were ready. The subject had been held in the utmost high level security and was now being escorted to the final area. As with earthly punishment, it wasn't a nice thing and only done in extreme cases but sometimes it was the only answer.

They were approaching the event horizon and this was the most testing part of the operation for a fraction too far and they would all be sucked in. The propulsion had to be done with minute accuracy with all the spirits acting as one, there was no margin for error. They stopped. On the command of the leader, they all used their spiritual force to shoot the evil spirit into the magenta hole. As with a black hole, the victim was stretched until it was no more and destroyed for eternity. The ultimate punishment, never to return in any form.

It is time for a moment to clarify certain aspects before continuing.

Remember, when a person in body looks at another, they see the human form but not what lies in the soul. So you could trust a person implicitly, but they could be putting on a façade while they take advantage of your kind nature. Likewise a murderer does not have it printed on his or her forehead so you don't know the hidden side.

Apply that if you will to spirit. Apart from people who claim they have seen 'ghosts' everyone can experience some form of connection if not by sight, by sense. How often have you had goose pimples and not known why, or known someone that you just knew wasn't right but you couldn't explain it. So when the spirits see or feel a presence, it doesn't mean they can identify it straight away. The higher levels have achieved greater powers which are put into use when required but that doesn't only apply to the good angels. The evil can be equally or even more powerful which is why the watchers are always on the alert for the slightest hint of danger.

Those of you who perform on stage will know that with costume and make up you can change your appearance completely and become the character you are playing. You are still 'you' and will continue to be so when you leave the theatre, but if your performance was good enough, the audience will have gone along with the act.

Again, the spirit world uses such tactics but with much more skill and can take on any role to suit the purpose.

So when Hannah wasn't sure if she saw John or not, Hope knew that another entity could have been taking his form and if not to a perfect extent, it would beg the question as to the true identity.

This may appear to be a clumsy way of operating but that's how it is intended, for it immediately casts a doubt but there doesn't have to be an explanation and the true identity remains covert.

If this sounds complicated, you will have realised that the earthly existence is fairly simply until touched by the spiritual, and not only just touched, but ruled by.

Another skill used by spirit must be mentioned here. Let's look at it from the evil side for a moment. Suppose one entity wanted to either infect a whole area or throw suspicion on the good angels, it would split into several images. Or it could just project itself or its malice to one or more people so the good forces would be chasing the wrong person or group.

Take the family. If they were good people, the evil would place a mark on them for them to appear a threat but if they in turn were bad they could spread themselves over quite a wide area depending on their level of skill. So the angels are never quite sure what they are observing.

Let us not forget the undercover operators. With the evil hovering around the area of the family it could mean that they themselves were the threat or they could be the receiver of an attachment. But either way, as already explained, the rule is always to keep a distance as intervention could hamper an even bigger operation.

Nobody welcomed Mondays. Denise and Sue were getting ready for work and Kieran was very reluctantly getting his things ready for going to the academy. John had a day off so wasn't going to hurry to get up. He was on nights from Tuesday until Saturday this week and weather permitting might potter around the garden. There was plenty to do and he liked a bit of quiet time.

"Don't forget to ring Mam." Denise called as she left almost slamming the door behind her.

"I will if I think about it." John turned over in the hopes of going back to sleep.

Sue was nearly at work when her mobile went.

"Oh god it's her." She muttered seeing it was Lisa. After a few rings she answered and before her friend could speak she gabbled "Can't talk now, late for work."

"Hang on." Lisa yelled. "I just wanted to say sorry."

"Well it doesn't matter really." Sue tried to sound offhanded.

"No, I was a bit shitty I know. How about coming round later?"

"I can't tonight."

"But there's two fit looking guys coming and…"

"Well I'm sure you can manage both of them plus any others who might come."

Lisa was getting angry. Nobody spoke to her like that so who did this upstart think she was?

"Well if that's all the thanks I get for trying to help…"

But her words were lost as Sue's phone was now off.

That hadn't gone according to plan. Lisa wasn't one to be fobbed off, she like to be the one giving the orders. Her current guardian watched with interest. He had been warned about her deviousness and knew that if he wasn't careful she had to power to throw him out along with the others. So this had to be handled very carefully.

She had been aware of his presence since the changeover and was rather drawn to him. There was a certain charm and she wanted to know more, much more. She referred to him as Pixel which was the first thing that came into her head, little knowing he had placed it there. Time for a little intimate conversation.

Having just taken a shower she stood there completely stark naked with a slight smirk on her lips.

"So what do you think?" She spoke aloud.

The reply shot straight into her head and was not audible.

"Extremely pleasing."

"Ooo, a smoothie eh? Well that makes a welcome change I must say."

Pixel was actually thinking "common little slut" but shut that off so she wouldn't pick up on it. He had been filled in as to her past and knew this had to be played with the utmost caution for they didn't know what they were dealing with, also she would have him removed the moment he put a foot wrong.

She wasn't going to mess about and asked where he was in the room. Normally she would have picked up his movements but this one was different and seemed to be all over the place but at the same time.

"I've been too long without a decent f..."

Before she could come out with her usual flow of unsavoury comments he answered.

"Right in front of you. Surely you must know that."

This could have caused a problem as she didn't like anyone to be in charge so he quickly added "Just teasing. I won't do it again."

Before she had chance to say or do anything he was caressing her in a way she had never known and there was no way she was going to throw him out now or for a long time to come. It wasn't the first time she had interacted with spirits this way and this one was better than any she'd known. So at least he had achieved one thing. He had his foot well and truly in her door, to put it politely.

When the higher angels had decided on this placement it had been a problem, for on the good side if Pixel could remain in place she would be closely monitored as to her intentions, but if he was keeping her happy, she may not spread her net and that was what they were waiting to know. They had opted for the 'on the spot' surveillance and sent an image she couldn't refuse. Pixel was fairly comfortable with this one although it did make him feel quite dirty when she was in full flow. He was glad he was in the male mode as he would have found it very unpleasant to be intimate as a female.

Although spirits are supposed to be sexless, they do have their preferences and some like to appear in one particular gender whenever possible, but work is work and the job has to be done regardless of any personal whims.

Something strange was happening. The evil uprising in the neighbouring towns seemed to be dying down for no apparent reason and the whole area was quite peaceful as regards spiritual activity. But nothing was taken on face value. Sometimes a visiting evil cell would place something for later use then leave, only to activate the device later. A complete scan was done but nothing seemed obvious. So that meant a search had to be carried out on the inhabitants for if they were the carriers it wouldn't show up on a land or building check. So the order went out for an immediate investigation.

What they found was worrying. There was no big evil deposit anywhere but there were tiny little shards in every person, animal, bird, fish, but no plants, trees or the like. So something was in position for all to bond at a given order. But there was another peculiarity. In the town where the family lived, nothing was affected. It was all completely clear like a little oasis.

The word of the latest 'magenta hole total' had spread through the higher levels and it always left a rather unpleasant feeling for no one liked annihilation but when it was executed it was the only solution for the sake of other beings.

A warning had gone out that another would soon be needed if the perpetrator could be identified, for something was lurking that need to be destroyed for good. It was in the town where the family lived but was so well hidden it was going to take some flushing out, and then it would take every ounce of concentration to bring it to justice for this wasn't a minor spirit out for mischief or revenge, it was a high order evil that had escaped the net every time.

The question arose again as to whether the family should be left alone in case they were good watchers trying to fool it into showing its identity, or were they in fact the evil itself. Difficult question which for now there was no answer. Patience was going to have to be used but there had to be a time limit as this couldn't just fester away indefinitely. There would be a concentrated watch kept on the place but from way up so as not to be detected. Everyone involved knew they were on a time limit, but for how long?

There were also a couple of Mergers hovering around the various towns but although they knew something was probably right under their noses, they couldn't pin it down. It was either extremely well masked or it was transferring its presence to other people or things. But these were highly trained spirits and wouldn't give up until it had been flushed out.

Another situation was arising that could also be thought of as suspicious but because it was happening at this time, the high angels knew the reason. Someone had gone missing in a nearby town. Nobody noticed at first because the man was a bit of a recluse and didn't mix much. It was only when the curtains were never drawn back that neighbours started to wonder. He didn't have milk or papers delivered so the fact that they hadn't piled up didn't arise. Someone ventured to call through the letter box to ask if he was ill or had fallen but there was no reply. When a house is empty, it has a different feel to it, not the same as when somebody is in but just doesn't chose to open the door. It was impossible to see anything through the letter box as there seemed to be a dark curtain over it.

Eventually the police were called and asked if the man had any known relatives or friends that might have a key but none of the neighbours knew of anyone. The fact had to be considered that he may have gone away and knowing the kind of man he was, he wouldn't have told anybody. It was difficult because you couldn't just break into someone's house without enough cause for concern. The police looked in every downstairs window and when a man brought his ladder, the upstairs windows apart from the bathroom were also viewed. Everything seemed in order. The man wasn't lying on the floor anywhere and there were no signs of a scuffle or a fall. It was decided to make a few enquiries but it was clearly stated to the neighbours that the man didn't have to explain his comings and goings. This didn't go down very well as the neighbours didn't think enough had been done.

But this wasn't an isolated incident. There had just been a similar case up north. Someone vanished without trace. In fact this happened all over the world but people rarely heard about it. If on occasion it did warrant a small paragraph in the local newspaper, people tended to put it down to the pace of modern living and comments like 'was probably overspent on his credit cards' or 'well she asked for it the way she carries on.' With every disappearance the reason was much worse.

Despite her pleasures with Pixel, Lisa was concerned she may have lost her contact with Sue. She had to stay in touch with the family and if she was peeved that her friend had blanked her. If anyone did the ignoring, Lisa did it, people just didn't do it to her.

"Oh give her a couple of days, she'll come crawling back," she thought. "When nobody else wants her."

But Sue had no intention of returning. If she wanted to know what Lisa was up to, she didn't need to be in physical presence. That's when Essie would go to work for she still couldn't fathom what this girl was playing at, apart from the obvious and keeping her distance might just draw her out.

Hope had been warned to keep the protection on high, because Hannah may not be in the direct firing line, but could get caught up in the backlash if things got too close to home. The guardian felt very strongly that the high powers knew exactly what was going on but were not divulging it for two reasons. Firstly they always kept secret information to themselves so as not to jeopardise any attack and secondly if innocent spirits weren't aware of what was happening, the evil couldn't home in on them to see what they knew, thereby putting them and their charge at risk. So it was necessary to often work in the dark but stay alert.

Kieran was quite well liked at the academy but had no really close friends. No one could accuse him of staying out of activities as he would have a go at anything and his tutors hadn't a bad word to say about him. But whereas most would have a close friend, he didn't seem to find the need. With it being mixed there was no shortage of teenage girls for him to get friendly with and he was regarded as very fit, but there was always a barrier. When any tried to get close, he stopped it dead by saying he had a girlfriend and didn't believe in being unfaithful. This led to a lot of speculation as to who it could be but then the rumour went round that she didn't go to this academy. After a while with various gossip adding to the mix, quite a picture had been built up even to her having a name. Kieran found this very amusing but it stopped any suggestion he was gay.

If it had been his choice he would have preferred not to have the attention for he liked to just be seen as one of the crowd, not paying too much attention to anyone, whereas he was always on full alert, and if there was anything disturbing the waves he was on to it.

He was picking up something unusual. The class had just returned from lunch and the atmosphere was different. There was something stirring the vibrations and the whole space had a feeling of unrest. Some started arguing, others would push a book on the floor just for the fun of it but this was not pleasant. Immediately Kane rose up to take stock of what was in presence leaving Kieran with his head lowered, just sitting at his desk. It was the smell that hit him first. Not a physical one but a spiritual odour that accompanies minor evil entities which proved this was not a high power, but what was it doing here? Maybe just passing and thought it would have some fun on the way.

Suddenly its attention was on Kane. It didn't like being watched and acted like a naughty child that had been caught with its hand in the cookie jar. He was about to despatch it when its mood suddenly darkened and the smell changed to an acrid stench that would make anyone heave. So was it cloaking it's true self under the guise of a lesser evil or had another taken over because it smelled danger?

The tutor entering the room caused a shock wave and the entity, whatever it was, vanished. Kane sank back into Kieran but retained the knowledge of the moment.

After a short reprimand about the noise the class had been making, everything carried on as though nothing had happened. Denise, John and Sue took the experience on board and stayed alert in case of another such visit.

Finch had been aware and had identified the visitor as a known troublemaker with only a moderately middle level of power that liked to create as much unrest as it could but didn't seem to have any connection with the family or anyone known to them, so this could be almost disregarded. Never absolutely, as nothing can ever afford to be ignored.

Chapter 5

The high levels were preparing for another Magenta Hole Total.

The man who hadn't been seen for days and whose neighbours had alerted the police had been removed. Unbeknown to those living near him, he had committed some of the vilest crimes imaginable and was about to suffer the consequences. His list of horrendous acts would have closed many cold case files and how he escaped physical punishment only proved how devious he was. But how did they dispose of his bodily remains?

Time for the strangest explanation you will have encountered so far.

You now know about the Magenta Hole and how the spirit is destroyed for eternity. But what about those who are still in body? The question has often been asked "Why not wait until they are naturally dead before the soul is totalled?" The answer is simple. They are too evil to allow them to finish that earth life and inflict their suffering on any more innocent people. Regardless of how many lives they have lived they will have no more so they may be deprived of several more visits.

Another question is "But how can the spirit world dispose of bodily forms?" The argument that matter can neither be created or destroyed, it only changes its form seems to support this.

The following is an explanation in simple terms but please remember you are being very privileged to read it, for it is not readily disclosed and you will not be given the full details as they are only for those who conduct this operation to know.

The body remnants will never be found on earth, but that doesn't mean they are not somewhere else. Therefore matter has only changed its form.

This has to happen in an instant for obvious reasons as no trace of bodily fluid or tissue must remain and clean up spirits have to cleanse the area completely after the event. No entity ever interferes while this process is taking place. Some have tried but to their cost. The body is terminated by a secret process and then certain spirits take charge of the different parts as each requires a special skill ie bones are not dealt with the same as muscle or fluid. As soon as one kind has been fragmented it is transported, followed by the others. There must not be even one tiny dust size particle left and the area is disinfected.

But where do all the fragments go? The answer is simple, to the nearest planet, Mars. Why is it known as the red planet? In spiritual terms it runs red with the blood of earth man. Thousands watched as the rovers examine the planet without realising what the dust is.

And here is the frightening part. Imagine if and when samples of rock or dust are brought back to earth on a Mars mission?

They will be returning the fragments of the intense evil that has been sent away from earth. That means the spirits would have to examine every sample.

And there is another factor that may tie in with this. Man must not go to Mars. It will be fatal and he will be obliterated. None of the scientists will listen and think it is a load of rot, they must reach out and put a man or woman on there. But when they realise their terrible mistake, it will be too late.

Coming back to earth. There is another important player in this process. A very high level angel has to act as earth dispatcher. That means they are usually someone already in the area who is given the order to terminate the subject but has to accept management for every single part of the operation. They may do the job for a specific period of time and then it is handed to another local spirit. In the event there are several offenders at any time, each one has a separate dispatcher and they all report to a chief who must co-ordinate the departures or every one would be flying off at once. It can resemble a busy airport except that there are no arrivals, or shouldn't be. Unless man cocks it all up.

The high spirits decided that, at this point, the space agencies around the world should be closely monitored and even though it may sound harsh in human terms, the possibility of anything being transported from Mars must be thwarted. Yes, it may mean taking lives, but the alternative could result in much worse, even the total destruction of this planet as we know it. Watchers were also now placed around the red planet little guessing what they were about to witness.

Spirits are often given orders which they don't understand but nevertheless they have to obey them for the knowledge is not for them to know and also any evil foe could pick up on their vibrations. Such was the case when Hope was told to guard Hannah closely. She dare not even wonder why, she just had to do it.

It was one of the days that Hannah helped out at a hospital. Most of the small towns only had a medical centre but the largest, the one nearest to her had a small hospital. It wasn't an A and E but they did minor operations and were sometimes used as an overflow for recuperation if the patient wasn't fit to go home alone. There was a pharmacy, a small shop and a little café where Hannah worked on a voluntary basis. She enjoyed it and it gave her a purpose in life. Although her family liked to treat her as though she was past it, she still had her wits about her and sometimes she had to admit she did wind them up a bit.

Fortunately, there was a good bus service that dropped her right outside the hospital and she always left plenty of time so that she wasn't late. She made her way to the little storeroom, took off her coat and put her bag in the little locker provided. As soon as she had put on her uniform tabard she joined Janice behind the counter. The two got on well and Hannah never felt so comfortable when another helper was there.

"Think we're in for a busy one today." Janice smiled.

She in turn liked Hannah because they were both workers and didn't leave jobs for others like some that came but didn't stay long.

"Well that'll keep us out of mischief." Hannah laughed as she sterilised her hands.

"Do you want to serve or take money?" Janice asked.

"Well I did the till last time so can I serve for now?"

"Course."

They weren't sure how the other teams worked but this system seemed to make it streamlined and they moved the queues quickly plus only one was handling cash. All the sandwiches and snacks were packed and the hot drinks were in disposable cups so no food was touched but the ladies preferred to keep to their method.

Hannah's attention was drawn to a middle aged man who seemed to be hovering at the edge of the tables. The café was not enclosed with one side open to the main corridor so he could have been passing but something didn't feel right. Hope too had already picked up on him and for some reason strengthened her guard. Janice followed her partner's gaze wondering what she was staring at.

"Him." Hannah nodded in the direction of the man but when she looked he had gone. Hope knew he had gone alright and not physically. She strongly felt he was a lurking spirit whose image was so strong, Hannah had actually seen it whereas maybe nobody else did.

It wasn't unusual especially at large hospitals with so many souls passing over, but this wasn't that kind of place.

The toilets were opposite the café and at that moment, Fred the handyman/cleaner came out of the gents. Hannah beckoned to him and he came straight over to her.

"Did you see a strange looking man in there? Bit scruffy. Looked furtive."

"No m'dear."

"You sure." She wanted to be certain.

"I'm sure because there was nobody in there when I left and the only one that did come in was in a suit. OK?"

"Oh, thank you." She still looked uncertain.

"Why, you lost someone?"

"No, No, um thank you Fred, it's just there was a man and he looked furtive."

Fred was a kindly soul and would help anyone and he didn't like to see her upset.

"Tell you what I'll do, while I'm going about my business, I'll keep a watch out for him. How about that?"

"Oh thank you Fred, That's very good of you."

It wasn't the fact he would look, it was more a case of him not treating her as being silly and imagining things.

Hope wasn't going to leave Hannah's side for a moment but she was able to do a distance search to see if the man had left a wake and sure enough there was a faint trace of the feeling he had produced when he had been observed. But something wasn't right. Not wanting to draw attention she couldn't call on backup so would have to work this one through herself. It only took a few moments to realise it wasn't male it was female.

To clarify one point, let's recap for a moment. In the spirit world gender is a very fluid thing. Quite often it is as though it doesn't exist especially in the very high levels who treat it as a basic thing and not needed for their purpose. Others like to keep to one particular sex and if they've just been in body as a male they will show themselves the same when in spirit.

So Hope now questioned why a female would appear as a scruffy looking male. It could only be to throw the scent, but surely whoever it was would know they would be identified. It could be a trap. By a secret route Hope requested an observer to come onto the scene so that it would draw no attention to her or Hannah. Immediately her request was granted.

Any information would not be fed to her directly but by the secret route then relayed to Hope via several experienced operators.

If this seemed to be an over kill of a simple appearance, the smell in the wake was enough to prove this was no simple playful spirit but a watcher of a very high level. Another puzzle was why Hannah was able to see it? That in itself could have set off alarm bells with the apparition unless that was what she was meant to do but that would be to draw any observers away from something more important. Utmost caution was now essential.

Hannah was serving a small elderly lady but as she was putting the top on a coffee the lady reached out and touched her hand.

"Be careful dear."

"Oh you get used to it although we do get the occasional spillage." Hannah smiled thinking the lady was just being kind but her reply held more than it said.

"You be careful." The emphasis was definitely on the first word.

"Oh, er oh thank you, you too."

It was rather busy but when the moment was right she said to Janice. "That lady was sweet wasn't she?"

"Ha ha, which one, with all this lot. Come on now."

“The elderly lady, just had a coffee.”

Janice looked at her oddly.

“No elderly ladies. You’d better get some glasses.” And laughed.

“Oh I thought she’d come to you to pay. She didn’t strike me as one who’d go off without.”

“Well not much we can do about it now.” Janice looked round the small seated area. “If she took it with her, its gone, and she’s not sitting drinking it, look.”

Hannah had to admit she was right but she knew she had served the lady who then made her way to the till. As if to answer she heard in her head as clear as before “Be careful dear.”

It was obviously no good saying anything else for fear of looking a bit silly and the incident had been forgotten as far as Janice was concerned.

But Hope knew. She spotted the spirit immediately as a watcher who could give the most realistic image even to materialising for a moment. So the upper levels knew something evil was in presence and needed observing so they had sent a messenger to warn Hannah to be careful. All they needed to know now was the identity of the female and what she was doing here.

Large hospitals are known for attracting various spirits especially with so many passings but the smaller ones are usually day cases with a very quick turnover so there is no need for anything to hover to await snatching a soul during departure. But they hover for many other reasons. If someone has done them a wrong, or even murdered them it has been know for the departed spirit to seek revenge and will not stop until it is satisfied the offender has been truly punished and that can span more than one life.

So if this entity had a score to settle, it could be searching various places trying to track down its prey. Not finding it at one, it would then move on to another until it ran it to ground then it could play cat and mouse with it until it had driven it insane. Hopefully this person seen by Hannah was just passing, but if that were the case, why would she have needed a warning to be careful. It did pose the question that whoever it was could be after her.

Wren and Finch had been feeding their computer, as they called it when they input facts into their shared knowledge then tried to make sense of it.

"There's a definite pattern." Finch has been looking at the family from a distance.

"I agree. You sound off then." Wren was keen to know if they had both come up with the same formula, although he guessed they had.

"Well," Finch began "Father works shift as a warehouse man, albeit a small factory but one of the group, doesn't stand out."

Wren decided to add to that.

"And Mother is a computer basher in a multi office block, again not too big but large enough to mingle."

Finch knew they were on the same track so continued "Daughter has a temporary job at a convenience store, not a manager, just a worker."

"And Son is at an academy." Wren finished.

"And the pattern is that they are all in fairly similar placings but not in the same towns. Each one is different."

"And Gran is also a volunteer at a small hospital but further away than the others, so the same only different.

Finch thought for a moment.

"You know she is the odd one out in many ways, I mean apart from having a separate guard, so she could be just the base that they all had to use.

Wren had been looking at the unimportant facts.

"She also doesn't have many friends. She goes a couple of doors away for a cup of tea with another lady on her own but they don't socialise."

"Then there's Lisa." Finch reminded him. "Why has Sue got so close to her? That's unusual, unless there is a definite reason for it."

"I've always thought she was keeping an eye on her but playing with her at the same time. I mean she's not the sort you'd choose for a friend is she?"

"Makes you wonder who is the predator there." Finch went silent.

"Well we know Lisa likes to think she's holding the reins, but Sue isn't the shrinking violet she would have her believe."

"You sound more like the Gran every day." Finch laughed.

Wren could see the funny side.
"Well I've been round old folk a long time."
Finch saw the humour but it didn't distract him from the task in hand.
They were quiet for a moment then both had the same idea. With rumours that there could be a magenta hole total imminent and it may not be a single, they almost had an instinct that they could be right in the middle of the targets.
Again the question, was the entire family on the good levels or were any of them about to be obliterated? And why? But that was information never divulged, so spirits had to speculate if they had been closely involved with any heinous activities but it was never confirmed.

Hannah had a mobile phone but she didn't use it much especially when she was out and about. She said she didn't think it was safe and people could snatch it but she carried it for emergencies. That's what she told the family for she loved playing the old dear they thought she was but she was in fact she was more 'with it' than they knew. She felt it vibrating as she got off the bus and though that she would wait until she got home to see who had been ringing then ring them back.
She'd no sooner got her coat off than her land line rang.
"Hello?"
"Mam are you ok? Oh thank goodness, I've been trying to ring you. I wish you'd answer your phone. I was worried sick."
"Hold your horses Denise. Now slow down. What's the matter?"
"Haven't you heard? There's been a fire. At the hospital." Everything was coming out in short bursts.
"You mean where I work?"
"Yes Mam, I do mean that. There was a fire in your coffee shop. You couldn't have been left long. I'm surprised you didn't see the fire engines. It must have been awful."
Hannah was a caring soul and had to ask, "Was anybody hurt?"
"I'm not sure, but I think somebody died. Mind you it could be gossip, there's been no bulletin yet just a brief headline, but you know how some make more of it than it is."

There was total silence. All Hannah could see in her mind was the image of the man and the lady who had told her to be careful. Had she escaped something? Was something looking out for her?

"Anyway, I'm alright but I can see how you must have felt. I would if it had been at your place."

After the initial shock they discussed how the fire could have started, how much damage was done and again about anyone being hurt or even killed.

"I'm keeping the news on Mam, I'll let you know when I hear anything."

"Thank you dear."

But Hannah was already on her way to check her mobile to see if it had popped up there yet. This was awful. Apart from the fact she would be out of a job she did care about any possible casualties.

Wren had sent a scout to see what had happened and check on any wakes that may have been left for a spirit could have either engineered the fire if it was capable or manipulated someone in body to do it. The result wasn't unexpected but still not welcome. A strong presence had been there but not the scruffy man image, it was definitely appearing as female. This posed the possibility that the original one Hannah saw may have been scanning the place for someone else, or come back themselves later. But in that case, they couldn't have been after Hannah or they would have known she wasn't there.

Finch cut into the thought. It would depend on what order had gone out. Maybe it had been executed correctly or it had made an almighty cock up for the victim who was being removed to the mortuary was Hannah's co-worker Janice.

Wren carried on the thought. If a mistake had been made, Hannah was still in the firing line and they would be back. Another question. Why would she be? There had to be a lot more to her than anyone had realised.

Chapter 6

Having touched on the dispatchers on earth, those sending the fragmented physical remains to Mars, it is logical there have to be receivers at the other end. Imagine all the evil dust just dropping anywhere then having a moon rover landing on it. But on a serious note it isn't as random as it may appear. At first the deposits were placed as they arrived, that is all the dust from one offender was together, much as ashes are strewed on earth but without the respect. Then it was decided that by some remote chance, evil could find a way of reforming it, in layman's terms, sticking it back together.

It has to be remembered that the good doesn't own any part of the universe, and the evil is pretty free to come and go where it chooses so it is obvious all this activity is monitored. Imagine if the evil were to join several sadistic offenders together and there is no proof they haven't in the past.

But even the high spirits are continually learning and the decision was made to spread any one person's remains over as large an area as possible. This wasn't the perfect solution because dust could still be collected that was from many people. Those of you with a weird sense of humour will already have pictured one person's leg along with another's brain etc. and it may sound strange but that is exactly what could occur. Evil is highly skilled as well although we would rather not believe it. So the extra watchers were not only observing everything inch of the planet but some were allocated to stay with each receiver constantly and others to witness every particle of disposal. It is not surprising that it has become known as The Devil's Graveyard.

Do you still want to go to Mars?

News was spreading about the fire and although it had been contained to the coffee shop which was now closed the rest of the hospital was running normally. In an area where everyone knows somebody even in the next towns, it was the main topic of conversation and the phones were humming. Lisa was trying to ring Sue to find out what she could as she knew her gran worked there but there was no answer.

Denise decided to go over to her mum's as she felt she had been putting on a brave face but must be a bit shaken.

"Oh I'm alright, you didn't have to put yourself out." Was the greeting she received but Denise went in and asked if her mum wanted a cup of tea. Immediately Hannah recalled the old lady and she stood motionless.

"Mam. Mam."

The voice shook her back to reality

"Oh sorry dear I was just thinking."

"Well I think you're in shock. Shall I get the doctor?" Denise was pacing a bit.

"Oh stop fussing, I'm alright. Um... did you say somebody had died?"

"Well I'm not sure Mam, you know how gossip is. Don't know yet. So don't you go worrying over it."

Denise had made a cup of tea anyway, regardless of her mum's wishes when the phone rang.

"Hello. Yes this is Hannah. Oh I see. Well yes I suppose I can but I don't know anything."

After a few more exchanges she put the phone down and looked at Denise.

"What is it Mam?"

"Well, they want to ask me some questions."

"Who does?" Denise was getting concerned now.

"The hospital I think, yes that's right but the police will be there."

"Then I'm coming with you, in fact I'll take you." Without waiting for any remark she phoned John and explained. He agreed immediately and asked her to keep him up to date as he was worried now. Kieran was home so he told him not to discuss it with any of his friends until they knew what was going on, and he messaged Sue. All this was of course play acting, they had all communicated on a different level and were in tune but that had to be hidden from snoopers.

The coffee shop manager met them in the foyer and Denise was asked to wait there.

"But I want to come with her."

"I'm sorry but we have to see her alone."

As Denise went to protest the manager cut in with "The sooner we get it done the sooner you can go. Alright?"

It was more of a polite order than a request but there was no choice of argument.

Hannah was taken into a small office and directed to a chair, the manager to sit next to her. The rather stern woman introduced herself as one of the hospital management but Hannah didn't take it in, she was more concerned with the policewoman who was also studying her.

There followed a string of questions about the equipment she had used and was it working alright. Had she followed all safety rules? How was it when she left?

She had no problem answering all the questions and looked from one to another wondering why they were asking her as the fire had started after she left. They seemed satisfied but then the mood changed.

"You were working with Janice we believe."

"Yes that's right."

"And you left before she did obviously, is this normal?"

"Well yes, she works more hours than I do."

She was now feeling uneasy wondering what was coming next.

"We are fairly certain that it was an electrical fault that caused the fire but of course it will have to be confirmed. The fire officer is on site now so then we will be certain."

There was a pause then the woman said very quietly, "One reason we asked you here I'm afraid is to tell you first hand that your colleague Janice perished in the fire."

"What. Oh no." Hannah's hands went to her face. "I liked her, she was so nice."

"You see because of this there will have to be a full enquiry so you may be asked things in more detail later."

The meeting had finished so the manager took Hannah back to where Denise was sitting and left her to explain. They both sat for a while in shock.

"I thought I heard someone had died, do you remember Mam?"
"Oh yes you did but I never thought of it being Janice, I mean I wouldn't have wanted anyone to die, but her, she was such a lovely person you know. It won't be the same without her."
"Can we go home? They don't want you any more now do they?"
"Yes please and thank you for coming. I don't know how I'd have coped on my own, with that…that news."

Hope had been surveying the surroundings while her charge was being questioned. She had asked a fellow guardian to check immediately after the fire for any wake traces and there were no new ones, yet there was still the faint vestige of the scruffy man/female as though it wouldn't leave. This had to have some bearing on the events. But what about the angel that had warned Hannah? It was as if she had never been.

The upper levels were getting impatient. They were pushing Wren and Finch to come up with some answers regarding the status of the family. If there hadn't been a tie to Hannah who had given birth to Denise, they would have thought it was one of those times that a group of spirits materialised. This is hard to be believe in earth terms but it is more common than most would imagine. But in that instance the person or persons have no connection with any other earth person. They just arrive in one place saying they have moved, usually from a distance so they cannot be traced.
Another factor is that, like the family, there is only one entity, no separate guardian angel.
Wren did raise the point "What if Hannah was also involved?"
"But she isn't an entire being." Finch reminded him.
"Doesn't have to be."
"No, she could have been used as a carrier, even without her knowledge."
After a moment Finch continued.
"What we all want to know is why. Why are they here now? What is their purpose?"
Wren finished it off for him.
"And on which team are they batting?"

That was the most important thing. There was a way to find out but only used in extreme circumstances and usually when they already knew if they were good or not. If evil they would be monitored but if good, they were blatantly told to divulge their plans, partly so that the other observers didn't impede them.

"If they are aware we are watching, they could start making smoke screens to ward us off." Wren suggested.

"And then we would be none the wiser, even less." Finch added.

There seemed to be nothing they could do at this point. The family went about their business like any other ordinary one except what one knew, the others did at the same time. All the normal conversation was still a front. Denise had only gone with her mother to act as the dutiful daughter but in fact she didn't care much about it as it wasn't in her agenda. Or was it? Nothing could be assumed for there was something going on, a bit like a military operation and nothing, and no one must get in its way or else.

Just when all seemed to be at a standstill, another bombshell hit the upper levels although it would never be realised by those investigating the fire.

Janice knew Denise, not in this life but they had been enemies across the years so spiritually they recognised each others presence now. It must be explained that they would not need to meet physically for them to be aware of the others existence.

This threw a new light on it but with it went another question, Had Denise in some way been responsible for Janice's demise, timing it for when Hannah wouldn't be involved? And is that why she went with her mum so that she could estimate what the authorities knew.

This didn't mean that she was the villain. If Janice was on the evil side, Denise just brought her to justice for old crimes.

The players in this act certainly knew how to hide their true purposes, but surely the truth would come to light soon.

Lisa knew she had to get to Sue somehow but her friend was still blanking her. She couldn't go round to her house, because she had never been told where it was, Sue had always gone to her. But she knew where she worked so she would go there knowing there couldn't be a scene or she might loose her job. Then she thought again. Sue had been telling her to try to work there so she could apply and if she was unlucky enough to get it, she didn't have to stay. Then she wondered about waiting for her outside when she knocked off but disregarded that as the other one might just walk off leaving her looking silly. After thinking for a moment she clapped her hands.

"Got it. Of course. It's got to look like it was accidental."

She was in her normal position, lying on her bed with her knees up playing with her phone. Sue used to say it was part of her hand. For some reason she hit the news and the reports of the fire were beginning to headline. It said that although it still had to be confirmed, it was believed someone had died. That was it. She'd use the sympathy vote and although there were no details she was clever enough to get round that one. It was too late today to bump into her by chance but there was another way to try. Still using her phone she messaged her.

"So sorry not to have seen you but as you can guess I'm in bits after what happened."

Sue hadn't blocked her and read it with caution. She didn't trust her and knew this had to be a scheme, for although she hadn't been in touch physically, she knew exactly what this person was like and had been waiting for her next move. She thought for a moment then replied.

"Didn't know anything had."

That took Lisa off guard. She had expected the "Oh dear what on earth's the matter" kind of reply.

"You must have heard. The accident. I'm in shock."

Still Sue wasn't taking the bait but had to act a bit dumb because that's the image she had portrayed.

"Sorry, don't know what you mean. Have you had an accident?"

She almost smirked as she pressed the 'send' button. Lisa really didn't know what she was up against and was getting frustrated at this stupid piece of shit.

"You must have unless you've had your head in a bin. The hospital. Didn't you say your gran worked at one?" While she was typing she was coming out with a tirade of obscenities.

"Oh do you mean the one where there was a fire? Yes I did hear." Sue had to stifle a laugh. When was Lisa going to realise she was being strung along?

Although she didn't reply with this she shouted to herself "For Christ sake. The penny has finally bloody dropped." Instead she put "Well, you know somebody died."

"Here we go," Sue smiled to herself. "This is what we've been waiting for. Time for a pity party."

"Well, it was one of my relatives."

She couldn't be more precise because the details hadn't yet been published, only the fact that 'someone' had perished.

Sue had her.

"Oh dear I am sorry. Who was it?" She answered but thought "Wait for it. This should be good."

Lisa didn't expect that. She was so thrilled at having thought up a brilliant idea but as usual hadn't thought it through. She gave the impression on the next message that she was sobbing.

"I'm sorry, it's so - oh – oh - um well I'm not allowed to say at the moment."

"Oh dear. Why?" It was handy to be a bit simple sometimes.

Again Lisa was having to think on her feet. She hadn't imagined it being this difficult but then with Sue she should have known.

"Well… because they haven't given the details yet and so we were told not to say anything."

"Oh I see. Who by?"

"Who by what?"

"You said you'd been told not to say anything." Sue was dragging it out now. "Who told you not to say anything?" She repeated for added effect knowing it was winding Lisa up.

There was a pause which was obviously while she thought up a suitable reply. When it came it was a gem.

"Sorry, I thought I was going to be sick. Can't talk anymore. Will call you tomorrow."

Sue laughed. She'd driven her into a corner. Did the silly thing really think she had put one over on her? Lisa of course had to wait until the reports were public before she even knew if the victim was male or female.

If the onlooker thought that Lisa was hanging onto Sue for a reason, it would be true because she was a lonely person. People soon saw through her selfish idle ways and dumped her. Also she liked her ciggies and booze but expected her latest chap to provide them. She only tolerated Sue because she could look down on her and felt she could manipulate her whereas in fact Sue was observing her in some detail and had her at exactly the right distance.

All this exchange was noted by many observers in addition to the family.

Wren and Finch were summing up everyone involved with any of the family including Hannah. Nobody was necessarily who they seemed to be and in this game it could be the most unlikely character that was playing the lead. They were contemplating that Lisa could be a watcher or even a merge and her obnoxious exterior was just a bluff. So they would have to monitor who she came in contact with, and not only in the physical. The ones who even connected with the family and appeared to be nothing out of the ordinary were under scrutiny and even the smallest clue examined. Mostly nothing came of the searches but it was always the one little thing that could lead them to what they were looking for and of course the watchers and mergers were not all good angels. Some of the highly efficient amongst them were from the most evil sectors.

Let us pause for a moment and answer an important question. What do you mean by communicating?

The first thing would be talking to someone, waving, smiling any thing that could be seen or heard. Years ago one of the top answers would have been to write a letter or send a telegram. Then telephones came into everyday use and from them evolved texts, messages, social media and even to sending live pictures of yourself.

But stop right there. These are all produced physically but take it a step further. How many times have you been thinking of someone and then the phone rang and they were on the other end. Yes, they made contact physically, but you didn't until they called, and you were already on the wavelength. You were waiting for them.

People have often said that they just knew something had happened or was wrong only to be proved right. In those cases they can look back and think "So that was what I was picking up." But how many times does it not get proven because nobody liked to say anything for fear of ridicule?

It doesn't even have to be someone you know. There are people who go to bed feeling they will die that night, but they wake up next morning and think how silly they were. Then a day or so later they hear that someone they know has passed over. They are the people who have to take the feeling of transition, to ease the souls of those who may not cope with it.

Let us return to the family of four.

We know that they are all on the same thought pattern and every time one of them experiences something, they are all aware simultaneously. In body they may talk to each other as an outward show of support but they have no need to. So while Denise was with her mother at the hospital the others knew exactly what was happening. In this case there was no need to relate to the others but they would have to for outward show. You never know just who is monitoring you at any time so defences must be on high continually.

The high levels see through the cover and if the operatives are on a very secret mission this would not be practical, unless they have been placed as decoys, drawing the attention to themselves while the main action takes place elsewhere.

Up to now Wren and Finch had found no spiritual connection to Lisa but she had to be there for a reason and must remain under surveillance. She must show her hand at some point and the fact of her trying to reconnect with Sue may be the start of it.

Hannah also was very much in the front line for attention. Either she was completely outside of what was brewing and merely a host to give birth to Denise, or she was a first rate actress. Of all spirits Hope should know the score so she was also being watched from a distance.

The watchers around Mars were uneasy so a warning had gone off in high authority. Several noticed a slight disturbance in the dust, just a movement at first then it stopped almost as if it were playing games with its observers. It was happening all around the planet so could it be something geological maybe solar wind. But this looked as though it was in an organised pattern, not just random. A new alert had just gone out that some were forming miniature whirlwinds which were building to little tornados lifting the dust and spinning it round thus moving it from its original placing. But it wasn't staying like that. Some of the whirls from different locations were joining up then falling to the ground.

Wren and Finch were now in touch with much higher levels for this had a lethal possibility. There could be an extremely evil force at work and it was controlling the planet. It was in fact reforming the very fabric of the bodies that had been deposited by the dispatchers. That was why the dust was coming from different sites.

Although it was speculation, the higher levels knew that the evil wouldn't stop there but having reassembled individual ones they could join them together into one terrifying being. And then where would it go? It was doubtful it would be returned to earth so would it just remain on Mars awaiting its first visitors? Also, how many such fiends would there be? It didn't matter how many times the planet was viewed by telescope or probe, the manifestations would remain invisible, for when not in use they would simply slide back into the dust awaiting the next animation. And man is blindly prepared to go and set foot on it.

Sue of course knew about Janice even before she was told and was still keeping quiet about it as far as Lisa was concerned. She was quite looking forward to the fact that when her so called 'friend' told her she would be able to calmly say she knew. It would be easy to do in her normal physical mode as she could give the impression things just rolled over her without having much effect. It had been very useful many times when people had tried to pry.

The news was out about a woman having died in the fire but details were not being released until all next of kin had been informed but at least Lisa had a sex to lean on. There was no good calling Sue as she'd be as work and not allowed to have her phone on her. So at lunch time she tried but still no reply. That meant she'd have to wait until she finished work.

"You have no patience." Pixel was standing in front of her.

"Where the bloody hell of you been?"

"Shouldn't you be up by now?" He ignored her question.

"Well darling," she snarled "if I was waiting for you for to be up, I'd have gone off by now."

He moved over her and purred in her ear "I'm here to guard you, sweetheart." The last word was loaded with sarcasm and disgust. "I'm not just a plaything you know."

"You could have fooled me."

He laughed.

She was quiet for a moment then turned on her so called sexy purr.

"You know, you aren't helping me very much. If you are so clever, why can't you do something about that wimp."

His mood changed and he seemed to grow in front of her which she found rather menacing.

"For one thing I am not your servant. I don't go round running errands for you. You want something sorting, you do it."

Her mouth dropped open but she was so turned on by this macho look and god, was he handsome? She tried to play the hurt little girl.

"I'm sorry. I forgot myself. Am I forgiven?" She was laying back on the bed now.

To keep his image intact and stay on this job he thought he had better do just that. So he did, he got on with the job in hand. Funnily enough Sue was the last thing on Lisa's mind for a while.

Hannah wasn't due to work until Wednesday and had been told that until the fire officers had finished their investigations and with the tragic happening, the café was closed for a while. She fully understood this and had been wondering if she felt she could go back at all with Janice not being there and it would bring back so many memories. But she enjoyed it and knew she would have to think it over very carefully. With not being an employee it was just a case of how she felt about it as it was run totally by volunteers. She didn't want to be idle and contemplated the possibility of doing the same thing elsewhere but there didn't seem to be any call for it at the local health centres and anywhere else would have been too far to go.

It was midday and Denise rang her to find out how she was doing.

"Oh I'm alright really. Don't you go bothering yourself."

"Shall I pick you up and you can come here for dinner?"

“No, I will be fine. I’ve got plenty to do here but thank you anyway.”

Her daughter didn’t push it. She was secretly pleased as she was quite tired and was looking forward to putting her feet up. Plus she had other reasons for wanting to be at home with the family. Sometimes they had evenings in, probably all doing their own things, but nevertheless were in presence and sometimes that was needed.

When spirits are in close communication they are always aware of listeners for every thought is monitored so sometimes they have an unspoken agreement that they send out a bit of useless information that may sound like a picking but is in fact pretty useless. There is no danger because the facts are real so cannot be suspected as red herrings, it’s just that the family have no interest in them but it keeps the snoopers busy for a while. On this occasion they would be very surprised if they knew who was going to be tuned in.

Lisa tried again to get Sue but as before there was no answer.

“Oh sod you then.” She threw the phone on the floor.

“What’s your problem?” Pixel asked.

“Keep your beak out.”

“Oh, something rubbing us up the wrong way. Hmm?”

The language that flowed from her mouth needn’t be repeated here but use your imagination.

Pixel answered her in the way he knew would wind her up even more. He was totally silent.

“Where are you? You stinking arse wipe. Are you still here?”

He would like to have said he would be there when she behaved like a lady but even the thought was highly hilarious to say the least.

“Oh go to hell and stop there.”

Again silence. She didn’t even seem to know that he was at the side of her which was curious. Either she was a lower spirit than he’d been led to believe or she was exceptionally clever at cloaking. He couldn’t afford to take any chances so played the waiting game for now. She could make the first move, and she would, for patience didn’t seem to be her strong point, physically or spiritually.

Wren and Finch had been watching the Lisa episode with interest. When someone in body could communicate that easily, they were usually very highly tuned which meant she was playing a game. It was also a possibility that these two were a distraction because some would find them quite entertaining and they certainly weren't acting covertly. Pixel was a very experienced guardian and although he wasn't a personal guard at present he was capable of adapting to any situation in which he was placed. He quite liked this arrangement as it was much more interesting than being tied to one soul for the duration of their earth life and you never knew what was coming next. He was well aware that Lisa would oust him the minute she was sick of him so he had to keep some kind of interest going to be able to monitor her.

That wasn't just the upper levels had been observing that evening for the family seemed to be attracting attention from some rather unexpected sources. To the untrained eye, each of the members had a guardian which would look pretty normal and of course that was far from the truth but high levels would know immediately that this was for a special reason. Hope had arranged a temporary stand in for Hannah so that she could go and visit them as something wasn't sitting right and she wanted to know what it was.

There are occasions when you feel that someone isn't acting in their usual way and you wonder if they are ill, or got problems they don't wish to discuss. All you know is that something isn't normal. This was the feeling Hope had and knew she had to see for herself as sending a messenger wouldn't be enough. She had to observe from afar, because the images of the pseudo spirits were there for anyone to see. After a short while she knew and left to return to Hannah but she had sent an instant message by a secret route to the upper level. It was a shock but in a way not unexpected as she had come across a similar incident many years before.

When we watch television programmes or read in the news about man's space exploration, it can be easy to think that things are only happening now because we know about it, and not that they have been going on for centuries and when you add the spiritual connection it becomes very different and things can take on an entirely new perspective. For example you will now look at Mars in a new light.

Let's just look at a question some of you will ask. Why was Mars chosen, why not the moon, it's nearer? Before you are given the answer just take a moment to realise you are still thinking in physical distance. The choice had to be a planet not a satellite. Imagine how the colour of the moon would have changed over the centuries if that had been the graveyard. And man has already set foot upon the moon, despite speculation, which means he would already have stirred up the dust and brought some of it back to earth. The moon was never a possibility. Although this kind of dispatching was going on long before the space age, in the spiritual world they were obviously looking ahead to the progress of exploration of mankind.

Another logical explanation for the use of Mars is that it is solid and for some reason they didn't want the remains sent to one of the gas giants or go nearer the sun, so Mars was perfect. It begs the thought that someday the hierarchy have plans for the deposits but we simple souls are not privy to that.

Chapter 7

Hannah couldn't rest. She was tossing and turning so having an early night didn't work. She lay there wondering whether to make herself a cup of tea but as soon as she thought about a drink the image of the elderly lady came into her head. Then her mind turned to Janice and tears came into her eyes. She could never have explained what happened next, for she thought she saw her colleague sitting on the end of the bed.

"Don't be scared. I'm not here to frighten you." The words were not audible but as clear as if they had been spoken.

"Janice." Hannah was bolt upright now. "I thought you, I mean…"

"It's ok. I can't stay long but they let me come to warn you."

"Warn me. Why?" Hannah wasn't surprised she was communicating with spirit in fact she was too shocked to question anything.

"It wasn't an accident. And it wasn't me they wanted."

Hannah's mouth was wide open but no sound came out.

"I have to go, they are after you and they will get you. I don't know who you are but…" She had gone. Her time was up and the guardians had whisked her away at speed.

Hope was back and at her side but Hannah wasn't aware of it.

"So they are showing their hand." She thought as she watched her charge slowly get up and make her way to the kitchen.

Wren and Finch weren't surprised that an attempt had been successful in getting through to warn her and they watched as Janice's soul left the area completely, her job done.

The question still was unanswered. Why would this ineffectual lady be a target unless it was an old score from a previous life that was being settled? She didn't seem to attract any of the bad spirits and so was she being used to get at others.

“The family!” Finch decided. They must be trying to flush them out so we see who they really are, but instead of going in directly they are using the mum as a lever.

“It depends though doesn’t it,” Wren added “as to which side they are batting. If the family is an evil cell, is Hannah so innocent and does she know nothing about it. On the other hand if they are good and have a mission, are the evil trying to take out the mum as a punishment, or…” he paused.

Finch finished it for him “…or is Hannah the threat and is actually after them?”

Up to now they had no proof either way but they knew that before long they had to get to the bottom of it or who knew what might happen?

The higher levels and we mean much higher, often surveyed the lower ones because situations could span across any of them so it was best to be forewarned. For example the family could be in situ waiting, so all they had to do was appear perfectly normal and act upon instruction. But the high angels knew that sometimes an evil perpetrator could hide under this disguise for as long as they wanted without being suspected. This normal looking family, remembering that they did not have separate spirits could in fact be one entity. It had been done before and nobody had guessed until it was too late. Hannah therefore could be right in the firing line if she even suspected the smallest thing and if an attempt had been made on her life, did they engineer it? If so, they failed which didn’t look very good on their part. It was more likely another force had intervened for some reason.

Lisa looked at her watch. It was late but too bad, she was going to call Sue and if it woke her, good. If she didn’t act soon this tie would be broken and she couldn’t afford for that to happen. Pity Kieran was too young or she’d have targeted him before now, and she’d have made sure he didn’t blank her.

“Yes?” Sue could see who was calling so she had best get it over with.

“Oh, are you ok only I was worried.”

“Why?”

"Well…. I didn't know if you were speaking to me."

Sue was going to play a game now.

"Well you must remember, my gran had a terrible shock, with her friend dying, you know."

"Yes it must have been awful but I…"

Sue cut her off before she could refer to her relative.

"Oh yes it was your auntie wasn't it. I'm so sorry, I wasn't thinking."

"My aunt, oh yes, terrible thing."

Now she was coming in for the kill.

"I suppose you had to identify her. How did you cope with it?"

This threw Lisa completely she didn't expect such a reply and Pixel laughing didn't help.

"Well, I …mean, well I didn't have to do it thank God."

"Oh. That's strange. You must have a cousin then."

"Cousin?"

"I'm sure I read her niece had to do it or could it have been a nephew? No it was definite a niece."

Lisa was getting, in her words 'thoroughly pissed off' by now. This wasn't how it was supposed to go. She was in charge so she should be asking questions not answering them. But before she could come up with anything, Sue was going for the jugular.

"I suppose it was with dental records or jewellery wasn't it, I mean you couldn't have identified her, I mean the way she was burnt. I'm so sorry, I didn't think."

Sue had to clap her hands over her mouth to stifle any noise that may have escaped.

"Well, as you can imagine I don't want to talk about it anyway they said I'm not to."

"Who did?" Sue smirked.

"Who did what?" Lisa was really in a corner and her mind wasn't functioning.

"Who said you mustn't talk about it?"

"Oh everyone. I need a fag."

Sue knew all along the woman was lying for attention and this had given great satisfaction to appear top dog for once although she had to be careful or Lisa would be suspicious as to her newly found confidence so she would have to go back to playing the down trodden boring friend if she was going to find out anything that she needed to know. She just hoped she had played the simpleton to effect.

"Well you handled that beautifully my dear." Pixel was an expert in sarcasm. "She was playing with you of course."

"I need a drink." She was feeling round for the last glass she had used.

"Oh I thought you said you needed a fag." He was winding her up now.

"I need a drink and a fag." She yelled. "Anyway what do you mean?

"About...?

"Didn't you just say she was.... Oh what the bloody hell was it?"

"Playing with you. Play...ing!!"

"Shut up or you can piss off with the others. I don't need guarding"

"Oh I see, you can carry out your mission on your own."

"Mission. What the hell are you on about?" She was quiet for a moment then said, "You two would make a good pair."

"We two?"

"Yes, you and her, that Sue, you could insult each other non stop and probably both enjoy it."

"Ah what a good idea."

"Bugger off then."

"Bye."

All went very quiet, then after a moment she called out "Ok game over, you can come back you useless dick."

But there was no reply, no movement or answer and she felt totally alone.

Even the spirit world doesn't always have an answer straight away and they have to send out the investigators, those who have to dig through tough exteriors to find out what is going on. When something appears in the slightest way threatening to any of the planets especially earth, and equally the spirit world surrounding it, certain forces spring into action.

A moment of explanation here. Obviously anything affecting the planets in the solar system would have a physical effect but also a spiritual one. This may not be to everyone's liking or agreement but please read it with an open mind. We like to think our loved ones are with us constantly but they also have work and they are not only tied to the earth. They can be with us in a second and leave a small part of themselves with us but can be working near another planet or moon. And they still have emotions. If they see someone they love who is deeply upset they may have to pull back to get themselves under control before they return to comfort them. They enjoy nothing more than to share in a relative or friend's happiness at special occasions or just when they can have a one to one with them. Unfortunately the living are not always tuned in and it must be very frustrating for the spirits who are trying hard to let you know they are there.

You will now have a slight insight into the greater picture. So among the workers are observers or scouts if you like who report by secret means to their superiors who then send highly experienced entities to take a closer look. As Mars was under constant observation due to the deposits, anything that was slightly different was reported straight away. Since the mini dust whirls the sentinels could sense that something wasn't normal but couldn't tell what it was.

It was time to call in one of the highest skilled groups, known only to the high authorities. They could move around undetected without leaving a wake or even disturbing the air, so nothing could trace their route. If they stopped at a certain place there was no space created in the area, they just merged with it. For purposes of identification they will be referred to as The Team.

They were now examining not only the areas where the whirls had occurred, but did a complete scan of the whole planet then returned to their base before anyone would have even guessed.

It was not good. Apart from the ground, there were minute traces of dust forming a helix and it was programmed in the direction of Earth. Obviously with the rotation of the planets this wasn't mapped in a straight line but without going into all the mathematics, the target was definitely Earth.

Questions were flying around. Was this the first or had this been going on for, well however long? Nothing was certain. But if it wasn't here, it soon would be and it could only be described as concentrated evil. The Team immediately tracked the dust on its journey as they needed to find out where it would land. Another question. Was it heading for a specific place or just set down at random? If it was going to a pre-ordained site there was a reason for it.

They also relayed the thought that in reverse to the despatching and receiving organisation from Earth to Mars, it had to be planned the same on the return. So a spirit on Mars had to send it but who was the Earth receiver? Who was now awaiting their next consignment?

Wren and Finch had been brought in confidentially and they asked if the dust was random or had certain villains been picked to return to Earth as their former selves. At the moment this was an unknown factor.

"Harbinger." Finch stated.

Wren was working this out.

"You are saying that apart from the receiver, there is a herald who informs them when a consignment is on the way?"

This was agreed by the higher levels who had already had the same thought but were they stationed on Earth or on Mars, or somewhere in between? They could be anywhere.

"They could even be on Enceladus for example." Finch was thinking of Saturn's moons, and even out as far as the Kuiper belt, the edge of the solar system.

"Would distance matter? I don't believe it would."

"Because they don't communicate in physical terms and as we've proved, a thought can travel for ever unless something gets in its path."

"Or it meets its intended receiver." Wren finished.

Although the high angels had already worked most of this out, they liked to witness the way these two interacted and you never knew if a little snippet might pop out that they hadn't considered.

They were waiting to see if these two came up with something they had been considering and sure enough Finch was the first to mention it.

"The ultimate answer of course…" he wasn't sure whether he was being presumptive.

"Go on." Was the instruction.

"We send the irretrievable souls to the magenta hole, so why not send the dust remains to a black hole?"

There was a distinct pause for a moment but this was what the high ones had been waiting for.

"Well done."

That was all and they were gone leaving the two almost in shock.

"What did I say?" Finch wondered if he had overstepped the mark.

"I think you voiced their own thoughts." Wren confirmed.

"It's a serious idea. I mean then there is no pairing of the soul or body with itself or anyone else. Complete obliteration."

Wren was musing. "Well it is now, I mean once the soul has gone through the hole, the remains are nothing. Oh No." He stopped.

"Exactly." Finch was ahead of him. "Unless a vagrant soul takes over the remains, the dust, whatever."

"So let's recap. The souls of the Mars dust went through the magenta hole. End of. But if the dust returns or is reanimated, what will be using it?"

There was no need for further contemplation. It was only too clear. If the dust was on its way to Earth, what was waiting for it when it arrived?

When Hannah woke on Wednesday morning she still felt drained. She should have been going to the coffee shop today and she still felt the sadness at Janice's demise. Then she remembered the visit, or was it? Perhaps she was dreaming but it seemed too real. Then it hit her.

"Oh my goodness, she warned me. Someone was after me. Oh I wish I could have asked her more."

She felt quite weak and made a cup of tea to get her mind thinking straight. Everything was going through her head but mostly who would want to harm her? It wasn't a good idea to tell anyone of this as they would think she was going off her rocker. Especially the family. They'd laugh.

Denise was trying to get Kieran up for school which was never an easy job, Sue had already left and John wasn't on until later so he could look after himself. She was making sure she had everything in her bag when something seemed to click in her brain. Ah, there was something she must do today but the feeling was picked up by all of them, including sleepy Kieran who was now instantly alert.

For no reason Hope suddenly had to put a strong protective blanket around Hannah. At times like this she never questioned it, just did it.

At the same time, Lisa sat up and almost like a robot got out of bed, went to the cupboard and reached for some special tablets. Pixel was there before her and knocked them out of her hand.

"Bugger!" She muttered and again put her hand out for the medication. Again they were taken from her and dropped to the floor where she immediately stepped on them.

"Ow, ouch," followed by a string of colourful words, she screamed as she hopped about trying to reach her foot which hurt but the pills had slid under the waste bin without her noticing.

Pixel was very adept at picking up visitations and equally good at clearing them out. But in the split second he had recognised the visitor that was trying to prevent her from overdosing. It was Essie.

Sue was at work but could also use her spiritual side simultaneously. She didn't have to go into a trance or sleep as it was part of her so could use it at any time but carry on with her physical appearance. And of course it didn't end there, the rest of the four knew exactly what had happened. They all knew Pixel and although had to accept he was a brilliant operator, were well aware that he also worked to his own rules. At first the high angels had tried to make him tow the line but he came up with such good results that in the end they decided to let him work to his own methods.

Wren and Finch were very interested onlookers as it was now becoming apparent that the family was from the good sector but on a secret mission so they could observe but not impede them in any way.

It also seemed that Hannah was maybe being used as a distraction. She was no threat in herself but what better way to draw the family's attention than to put her at risk. In the meantime, the slightest lapse of attention may be all they needed.

Another point was considered. If the family were in fact one entity, there was no leader amongst them and any action by one of them would appear to the observer to be with the knowledge and agreement of the others. Sometimes this method was used in times of severe conflict. Send in one force however powerful and if it was obliterated, there was nothing left. However, divide it into any number of sections and if one was taken out, the others filled it. They didn't just take on the position, it was actually occupied.

Let's use a simple example. If you have ten pots of sand and someone comes along and empties one, the others don't all give a bit to put some back in the pot and diminish their own quantity, the tenth pot is completely refilled so all are on full power. That is the same in spirit and those, like the family occupying human form at the time. So if say, Sue was taken out of the picture, another would take her place but with a different name. A cousin would appear so that the force was complete.

You may think that although Sue's body had gone her spirit would still be active, but that isn't the way. There has to be another human form for various reasons. Sue as Essie may be recalled or even taken over for the time by an evil force.

Having decided on the family and Hannah's positions, attention was now turned to Lisa. They felt she needed watching and why was she so keen to curry favour with Sue. She must need her for something but it didn't necessarily have to be bad. There didn't seem to be anything hostile hovering around her space, and apart from good entertainment, she didn't seem to have much else to offer. Pixel was a skilled operator so he would dig out anything if there was anything to find.

The day had been pretty uneventful but something was definitely in the air. John was on the night shift and getting ready to go to work. Although he liked walking he preferred to drive when he was on late. He parked his car and made his way to the clocking in section. There seemed to be a bit of a queue which was unusual.

"What's up?" He asked one of his mates.

"Some bastard has done something to the machine, seems to be covered with some dust or something. Ray's gone to get a cloth."

John laughed. "Well a peck o' muck never hurt anyone."

“Bit more than that, it’s all over the place. Never seen it before.”

Ray came back and tried to clean the dust off the machine but it seemed stuck to it.

“Do you know,” he said for them all to hear “I could swear on my life that it wasn’t there when the last shift went off or they’d have said.”

Everyone was trying to get close enough to peer at it but Ray suggested they didn’t touch it until they knew what it was.

“Could something have leaked from up there?” John pointed to the roof.

“Can’t see anything.”

The shift manager joined them wanting to know the reason for the hold up. After Ray had explained and pointed to the machine he said that it had been alright when he came in earlier. He told them he would mark their cards to say they were in and they could get on with their work without further delay. Someone from maintenance would have to attend to it.

They had been working for about an hour when Ray walked off the floor. Everyone assumed he’d had to go to the toilet so didn’t give it any thought. When he’d been gone quite a while, John said that it seemed strange and wondered if he was ill. The shift manager said he’d go and see but was muttering under his breath and when he came back he looked bemused.

“Well I don’t know where the prat is.”

It was nearly tea break and one or two decided to have a scout round to see where Ray had gone. He wasn’t one to shirk his duties and would never have gone off without telling someone, but there was no sign of him so they had to get back to work.

About half an hour later he walked back onto the floor as though nothing had happened. But something had.

“You been under the sun lamp you old tosser?” One laughed.

Ray looked down at his hands. They had gone a strange pale orange red shade.

“Where have you been? Are you ill?” The manager wanted to know but stopped suddenly. “That doesn’t look right. Could it be catching? Go to the medical room, now.”

Fortunately there was first aid cover around the clock and tonight a former male nurse was on duty.

“My god man. What have you done to yourself?” He beckoned Ray to sit in a chair while he peered at his face.

“It’s my hands.” Ray seemed bewildered.

“I know and it’s also on your face, your neck.”

The nurse was keen to know if it had spread any further and he’d never come in contact with anything like it before.

“Um I’m not sure.” Ray was looking weak.

“Well I think you had better go and get checked out at A and E because I don’t like the look of this at all.”

But Ray was giving him a strange look.

“Where I go, you go.”

“No, I don’t think you understand. You could be contagious. You mustn’t touch anyone or have them touch you. Now do you understand?”

Ray was on his feet and before the nurse could move he had him round the neck, moving his hands over any exposed skin he could reach.

As soon as he had done with him, the colour vanished off his own skin but had transferred to the nurse who now lay on the floor.

When he returned to work the lads wanted to see how he had got on.

“Brilliant, they gave me some stuff and it took the inflammation straight out. Look.” He bared his arms for all to see. “I feel great now.”

There was a bit of banter about him having had a rest but now he could do their work as well. It was all taken in good humour and everything was soon forgotten.

But in the high levels it was major cause for concern for here was proof that the dust had indeed been transported. Ray would now be infected with evil as would the nurse and anyone else either of them touched. So it wouldn’t be a straight transfer of one to another it boded a mass epidemic and evil would intend to win.

While John physically stayed at his work station, as Jay he was watching the scene in the medical room. He had already examined the clock and surrounding area and so as John he knew to give it a wide berth. The rest of the family were on full alert as they fully expected to witness a similar incident at any time.

Wren and Finch were also witnesses from a distance and knew that this was what the higher angels expected although not which form it would take.

"It's almost like germ warfare." Wren thought.

"Now it's got a foothold, there will be no stopping it." Finch was worried but suddenly came up with an idea.

They sent a message to the high levels and immediately they were in conference.

"What are your thoughts?" The hierarchy already knew and had made plans but wanted to see just how sharp this pair was.

Finch started by saying "What has been returned, can it not then be sent back to Mars."

"Can't we dispatch it in some way, similar to the original method?"

There was a pause.

"That seems the obvious answer. But then it would just come back."

Again a pause while they waited for one of them to come up with the obvious.

"Black hole." They chorused.

Wren continued "Any dust or whatever form it comes in is immediately waylaid and sent there."

"Before it reaches Earth." Finch added.

That was what they wanted to hear but there was a problem. Because they had to wait to see if it was in fact the plan to return evil to Earth, it meant that what had already been deposited would grow and spread, so although they could redirect any future consignments, they had to deal with this problem now.

"We won't know exactly where it is until we have done a wake trail." Finch stated.

It was confirmed that it had already been taken in hand by The Team and this time any trace would be destroyed and the Earth cleansed of this particular source. It didn't mean all evil had been obliterated, just the red dust.

Kieran was watching a program he'd recorded about the Falcon Heavy rocket for putting man on Mars. He couldn't sleep and was aware of the dust incident at John's work. He, as well as others knew that nothing could stop human man trying to push further into space, into the unknown, but they didn't realise that it was more than just the tactile element they had to deal with, for there is more to study and fear than pieces of rock brought back to Earth or examined as they take their course through space. For what we refer to as space, as some already know, is just as occupied by the spiritual as the physical. It is not empty or quiet or still and although man has achieved great things and learned so much, they have barely touched the surface. And some things they will discover will be unbelievable and take a lot of understanding but that is in the future.

Having now ascertained that the family were good angels on a secret mission or observation, another next question had to be answered. Where did everyone else fit in the picture? The immediate candidates were Hannah, and Lisa. They didn't think Pixel had any part except guarding who he was allocated but you could never be sure.

To recap on Hannah. Up to now she had seemed an innocent bystander who didn't get involved spiritually and had just been placed to produce one of the four. While this could be a very elaborate cover, it seemed likely she would have shown her hand by now.

Then there was the question of Janice, and not only her warning but the old lady in the shop. Why would anyone be out to hurt Hannah if she wasn't a key player, unless it was to get a route to the four? But if any evil thought that by killing the mother the family would be distraught they were out of their league for the family may be in body but working very much in spirit.

Lisa. Now here was an enigma. She seemed a complete waste of space and resources. She was well in tune with the spiritual as was evident with her interchange with Pixel, and they went back a bit. Also why was she so keen to keep in contact with Sue? She had given no inclination of knowing about Essie even when she was in her flat getting the pills out of the way unless of course she didn't intend to. It was only a fleeting visit but would have been enough for the trained entity to spot. That was a fact that the high spirits must keep on board.

Wren and Finch had also been going through this summary hoping something would jump out and grab them, but these events could go on for ages without anything being proved. The players were all top league and wouldn't give anything away if they could help it. Usually it was a case of driving one into a corner but even that was not as easy as it might appear.

"You do realise that in the family there is a newcomer. One not so experienced." Finch had been doing a bit of digging.

"Well, they're all pretty high standard. Do you mean Kieran?"

"No. Don't be fooled by him, He's lying low for now."

"Well Denise seems to be running the show." Wren was going through each one.

Finch seemed amused.

"Correct, but that leaves the other two." He was wondering if Wren would come up with something he had noticed.

"You mean John don't you?"

"Absolutely. The others would have spotted the dust before it got to earth and landed on the very piece of equipment he was about to use, which was why it was aimed at him."

Wren was a bit puzzled on two counts.

"The first thing is that if it was aimed at him then it would also be targeting the other family members, maybe not immediately and not in the same form as that would arouse suspicion."

"Carry on."

"Well as you said the other three would have noticed it long before. He didn't even notice until somebody else did, but he should have been the first." Then after a pause "Unless he didn't want the evil to know he'd seen it. It would be too obvious and draw attention to him."

Finch soon squashed that idea.

"Forget that. It wouldn't have mattered who'd seen it first because they all would know as soon as the first one spotted it. So there was no need for false secrecy. No, I don't think he was aware, or he was and there was another reason for him not speaking out."

They were both lost in silent thought. This put a new light on things. Wren broke the pause with a very serious new slant.

"He was expecting it and..."

"Go on." Finch was very serious now.

"Is he the receiver?"

If they had traced the receiver, they also had to locate the dispatcher and the herald.

Chapter 8

The work was nearly finished in the coffee shop and Fred was told to make sure everything was ready for re-opening. There was to be no fuss due to the tragic happenings so there would just be small notices around the place informing people of the date.

The closure had been a blessing in some ways for Fred was also able to do jobs in the toilets that had to be put off due to the continual usage. He was in the one marked ‘disabled’ and had a strange feeling he wasn’t alone. For some reason he opened the door a bit and wedged it with a waste bin. Somehow he felt safer that way. But the feeling was still there and it wasn’t nice. He wished he could have used one of the little wooden sticks his late wife was keen on that cleared the atmosphere of negativity. She was really into that kind of stuff. The only trouble was you had to light them then wave the smoke around and that would not be a good idea! Imagine setting off the smoke alarm after recent events. The presence was still there and there was no doubt it wasn’t good. Suddenly he sensed he could smell the smoke from the sticks and after a moment the atmosphere was calm again.

“Thank you love.” He whispered for he knew she must have helped him and the smell had now gone.

He’d never been one to go in for ‘strange stuff’ as he called it but he hadn’t objected when his wife took an interest in various crystals and other things. As long as it kept her happy. But now he knew she had been watching over him and he didn’t feel alone.

As he gathered up his tools he thought “Maybe not so daft after all.”

Fred was one of those people who had experienced a few strange happenings in his life but hadn’t dwelt on them or discussed them with anyone. What he didn’t realise was that he was very much in tune spiritually but didn’t recognise it and put things down to coincidence or a bit of intuition. He reckoned that with experience of life you got wiser in your old age and that did him.

But he was one of those that is employed when necessary and unbeknown to him the higher levels had used his connection to materialise the old lady to warn Hannah. Having seen the scruffy man/female they knew they had to take action and fast, sadly to Janice's cost.

It is sometimes best that communicating spirits don't realise they are being put in that position, for the lack of awareness can be useful barrier against snoopers. When the job is finished the memory is deleted from the person's awareness, therefore Fred would never know what had happened and the operators always made sure they were out of sight when the task was in progress.

One thing had baffled Finch.

"Why did the scruffy man allow himself/herself to be seen?" He voiced to Wren but he had no answer at the moment.

And they had to remember the Hannah involvement and all the questions they had raised regarding her. A sweep of the place had come up with no lasting trace of any visitation except the man/female, whoever that was. At the moment this didn't seem to have much bearing on the Mars issue, but there were questions still to be answered, but that in turn would result in more questions being asked.

It was Thursday and the café was going to re-open on the following Saturday. Hannah had received a call asking her if she was fit to go back and could she cope with it. She was emphatic that she must go back and had no fear even after the warnings. The manager told her that they had decided on new tabards for the staff which should make it a bit easier for her and she was grateful for that. Also she was going to have a new helper that she could train, a young lady who seemed very willing so she wouldn't be alone.

As she put the phone down she knew it would be a bit traumatic at first but better to get the first day out of the way then she could start to enjoy it again. Her mind turned to her new helper. Strange for a youngster to do voluntary work when she could be out earning a wage. Perhaps it was work experience but then a thought hit her.

"I hope they aren't paying her."

It was a possibility and typical. Keep the willing older ones on free and pay a younger person who needed the money. Of course this was all conjecture but people's minds do run away when given the chance. But she would have to see what happened and it would be good to get back into the routine.

Denise was concerned about her husband going to work that night.

"Be careful what you touch." She warned him as she packed his meal into his work bag.

"Will you stop fussing? It's all over and done with." He seemed a bit tetchy as she put it.

"Well, just be careful."

John didn't say but thought "You just said that."

All this could be picked up by any passing listener which was just what it was intended to do. They had to appear to be a normal family, arguments, fussing the lot, and they were well experienced at it so it would have to be a very top notch entity to see through it.

Secretly Denise was concerned about the dust incident but she didn't let her thoughts dwell on it apart from wifely concern.

There are times when the only way to deal with something and obliterate evil is to take what appear to be very harsh measures even at the cost of earthly life. To prevent the possibility of evil spreading, the nurse from the warehouse had to be terminated. It was left to The Team to deal with it and within a short space of time the evil had been disposed of and the nurse had suffered a fatal heart attack.

The family knew before the news reached the warehouse and John was visibly shaken but Wren and Finch wondered if that was because of the death or the fact that the evil had been destroyed. At the moment it was debatable.

Kieran was still locked away in himself but the family never queried things like that. It was a known fact that sometimes one operator would be given extra tasks or they would have to study information released which could be detrimental to their current purpose and get rid of it. The topic at the moment of course was anything to do with Mars, in fact it seemed to be the main problem on all sides. The evil wanted to take charge and felt they were at least one step ahead, whereas the good angels had to thwart every attempt even before it was executed.

When plans are in operation the main problem is secrecy. It would be lovely to think that it could all be sorted and carried out without any problems, but that just isn't the case. If anything is going to be successful there are so many factors that could jeopardise it so they have to be squashed as the plan progresses. Basically in the spirit world there is little that is unknown so major incidents have to be controlled from as high up as possible. Then just the orders of that moment are issued and must be carried out without question even if they seem to have no bearing. No one on the front line knows the whole picture and that is essential.

The plan now was to send everything on Mars to a suitable black hole, not just the deposits for they could have contaminated the rest, but everything that was movable. The ideal outcome would have been to send the planet itself and before anyone scoffs, the size is not important, it is tiny compared to what is out there, but it could upset the solar system and of the rest of the planets. Also the problem would be as to where to dump the dust that is currently sent to Mars. It wouldn't be practical to send each few to a black hole, it would have to be done in quantity. All this has to be taken into account and the reason is because evil must be destroyed.

Pixel liked a challenge and always expected to win. He was very supercilious and almost preened himself in a way some found most objectionable. It was generally accepted that he was extremely good at what he did and always got a result. If he was given a simple task he was fed up within minutes as it wasn't rewarding. He had worked in company with Lisa a few times, sometimes totally in spirit but on occasions like now, when she was in body. Pixel was never in body now and was glad those times were over as he found them distasteful. He liked to be free.

He was now having to account to his superiors about his charge as nothing much seemed to be happening and he should be guiding her to a more productive life. He had no comment to make on the last issue.

Then they made him take notice. He was told that things were about to change and he must be ready and that help would be standing by.

"Help?" He almost screamed, spiritually of course, "When do I need help? I am perfectly capable of handling this, thank you."

There was a pause which he knew meant something serious was to follow.

"As we are not sure of the outcome at this stage, it is essential. That is all you need to know. Keep your senses tuned."

He would not have admitted that he felt as though he had been put in his place, but that was exactly what had happened. The high angels could soon knock the self importance out of him.

He hadn't left Lisa's place during the meeting and was still playing the silent role. He watched her now, a scrag of humanity. She could have had this span of earth life in front of her and what was she doing with it? Throwing it away when some would have given anything to be in her place with her chances. Time for action.

He moved her back to her bed and pushed her down sending her into an induced sleep. She was in a terrible place going down a flight of steps into a chasm. All she could hear were howlings and crying and the whole place was filled with doom and utter sadness. Suddenly she saw a hand in front of her.

"This is your last chance." The words were in her head.

What did this mean, her last chance? Last chance for what? As she felt a current of power pulling her down she reached up towards the hand which grabbed her and tugged to get her out of this nightmare. Up, up she went and gradually there was a flicker of light which grew brighter and suddenly she was lying on a soft bed with hands caressing her face and soothing her whole body. She sensed she could smell delicate fragrances wafting up her nostrils and she was at peace.

She saw people. Some were going down the stairs into the dark others were floating in the light all doing different things and looking happy. Then came the crunch. She heard a voice calling her name.

"Lisa, Lisa. Make your choice. Which way are you going? This is your last chance, for eternity."

The last two words made her jump.

"No." She cried out loud. "Not down. I don't want to go down."

"Then you must make a promise." The whisper was in her ear.

"Promise?" She didn't understand.

"A promise to yourself. That you will use this precious life you were given and not destroy it. You can do it."

A wave of utter despair was wafted over her followed by a euphoric feeling that everything would be alright. It depended on her. The two emotions were swinging to and fro like a pendulum in front of her until she could stand no more.

"I'll do it!" She screamed as she sat bolt upright.

All was quiet and the room was empty, almost.

"Thought you would." The familiar voice made her furious.

"You!"

"Well someone had to."

Pixel moved close and put a gentle arm round her before he came in for the kill.

"I've been so upset watching you, in fact I asked to be removed."

"Why?"

That was the reaction he wanted.

"Because I hated having to watch you destroy yourself. You are worth so much more and I wanted you to make the decision to do something positive. You have a life. I am watching many now who would give anything for another hour, even another minute." He let the sound crack with emotion.

"Even babies?"

He knew he was winning although it was a tough method.

"Especially babies, and their parents."

"Oh my god, what have I done?"

He let everything sink in for a moment knowing he'd achieved his goal but he inwardly thought "Stupid bitch" which was nearer to his true self.

"How do I start? Look at me."

"Rather not thanks." He knew this would kick start her into action.

"Ok Mr Know it all, you can piss off now. A lady likes a bit of privacy."

“Yes m’am,” he sneered, “but make a good job of it because… I’ll be back.”

She felt the room change as he left, or so she thought, but had he? Guardians do not leave even if they let you believe they have. She should have known this, but her thoughts were on the new Lisa now and there was no stopping her.

When Wren and Finch and the hierarchy were deciding which black hole would be the one to use, it didn’t have to be the nearest in earth miles or even light years for in the spirit world everything is different. Distances can be crossed in seconds. For example the Milky Way galaxy is about 180,000 light years in diameter but in spirit that could be just a blink. This is where you have to think differently. It isn’t a case of when the next space ship arrives and they all climb aboard. It is instantaneous but there is no return. This was going to be an assignment that needed to be handled with utmost accuracy as the evil was hardly going to sit back and watch and do nothing. Also they wouldn’t be able to use to same hole continuously for the same reason and with evil intervention this arrangement may not be permanent and new methods would have to be considered. But that was in the future, what mattered now was the destruction of the current dust and surroundings.

Another question was discussed with some of the high angels. Supposing the family were good and on a mission, How could John be a receiver for the evil? There could be several answers.

He was an interloper who had fooled them into thinking he was from the good sector, but that would have surely have been suspected by the other three family members.

He was originally good but been used recently without his knowledge, ie brainwashed.

The worst, the whole family were an evil cell with a special target

This almost brought them back to square one but with added complications. They decided upon an unusual step. It is a fact that the extent of high angel levels is an unknown quantity. Some think it goes on indefinitely but there must be some who know if the family are good and must not be hindered. The only way was to send requests to the higher ones than say, Wren and Finch, who in turn would send as high as they could until an answer was received. The problem was, that if it was top secret, none of them would receive confirmation for fear of jeopardising the whole operation. It kept coming back to that issue all the time. So at the moment everyone must be on full alert and pick up on the slightest thing that seemed the least bit unusual or different to what was expected.

Although the sadness of the news about the nurse brought a cloud over John's place of work, everything else seemed to be going on in a normal fashion. There was no more dust or anything suggesting evil was at work there.

"I don't think he could have knowingly been a receiver." Wren suggested but Finch soon put a damper on it.

"May have been a tester."

"Hang on. Are you saying John's completely innocent, or he was used that once?"

"Keeping an open view. It would be a bit stupid to follow on with another attack wouldn't it."

"Right."

"Can't see any threads on him." Wren had done a scan to see if there were any permanent connections to his body or spirit but all seemed clear.

Finch was very quiet which always disturbed Wren because he didn't know just what his partner would come out with next.

"Been blind." Was the result.

"Explain."

"Where has our attention been?" Finch didn't have to say more.

"Oh barnacles!"

They both knew that this could well have been one of the red herrings used to draw their attention to one place while the real attack was somewhere else.

"Must ask the rest of the crew."

Finch often described their fellow spirits in this way. Apart from minor incidents, nothing of this scale had been noticed so was the evil playing with them? It could have them running about in all directions but still not actually carrying out its eventual plan.

"But we are sure that the dust is already here aren't we?" Wren was summing up but he was brought up to a halt at the friend's reply.

"Are we?"

"You mean, we have been conned."

"We know something came."

"And if we think we have destroyed it…"

"We will think we have won. And the door is open for them to carry out their full plan."

"It's always the uncertainty." Wren said.

"Always was, always will be."

The very high angels were also aware of another factor. Man. If the red dust was transported to a black hole the colour of Mars would gradually fade and would be noticed from earth. Man in his wisdom would then send up more Rovers etc to see what was going on and that would not only impede the removal but those on Earth would want to know what was causing it. That must not happen. In some way anything now destined for Mars would have to be terminated regardless of what it was carrying. But how long before Man would get the message?

The next couple of days were pretty uneventful and life seemed to tick over with nothing out of the ordinary going on. The spirit world was a hive of activity for the happenings around this area were just a part of what was going on continually.

Hannah had mixed feelings about returning to work but she was the sort who had to carry on no matter what. She was doing the ten till two shift which covered the busiest part of the day. She got there early and found her new tabard hanging up on her locker. It was mauve which she liked and as she put it on, it was as though two arms came round and smoothed it down for her. It wasn't unpleasant and quite comforting. Strangely it didn't upset her and she felt a feeling of calmness.

"Oh I'm glad you are here Hannah." The voice shook her from her reverie as the manager arrived with the new helper. "This is Louisa, I'll put her in your hands to show her the ropes." Then turning to the woman behind her said "This is Hannah, very experienced lady." And with that she was gone.

Hannah now had a full view of Louisa. Barely out of school wearing what she called the latest fashion consisting of ankle boots with narrow heels.

"Hello. You can put your things in there." She pointed to the small locker. "Have you brought any more shoes?"

"No, why?"

Hannah gave a short laugh. "Well we are on our feet all the time and, well, you could slip on those."

"What I always wear dear. It's the fashion you know." She looked at Hannah's sensible footwear and gave a little smirk.

This was going to be interesting and the guess was that she wouldn't last a week.

Then something else was rather obvious. Louisa noticed Hannah staring at her nails.

"Nice aren't they? Of course they aren't real."

"Oh?"

"Nah. Couldn't afford them. These were a pressie. Stick on."

"Well I hope they don't fall off." Hannah was not impressed. "Would you like to put your tabard on please?"

"My what? You don't seriously think I'm going to wear that." She pointed one of her nails at it.

Hannah had now had enough.

"It's the rules. We are dealing with catering. We all wear them and these are new so I suggest you wear it."

Someone with a bit more about them would have told her in no uncertain terms to get it on and shut up, but Hannah wasn't like that and the new girl had picked up on that straight away.

After a few moments of being stared at, she reluctantly took the garment and put it on.

"I hope to god nobody that I know sees me. I'll never live it down."

"It's not what you wear, it's how you wear it." Hannah said under her breath. "Well I will show you what to do. You can serve the food, it's all wrapped but you have to make the drinks to order. And before we start, wash your hands and then we have to use this special stuff, it's a sanitizer."

"Bloody hell!"

Hannah turned to face her. "Now look here Louisa…"

"For Christ's sake will you stop calling me that, I'm known as Lisa."

For a moment neither of them moved. Hannah recognised the name but thought it was too much of a coincidence. She'd heard Sue speak of a friend but didn't know much about her and this didn't have to be the same one. Anyway that girl wouldn't have been doing this kind of work.

"Something the matter dear?"

The voice broke into Hannah's thoughts.

"No, umm no it's alright, it just sounded familiar that's all. Common name nowadays."

But Pixel knew that Hannah was suspicious, probably only the fact that Lisa maybe being paid, but he would have to keep a close watch as this could turn unpleasant and not quite what he had anticipated. However, circumstances could always be changed and with this girl on the scene he knew she had found a back door to get to her objective, Sue.

Wren had been observing all this with interest. This was a quick turnaround for someone who, shortly before didn't seem to give a damn about herself or anyone else, except for keeping in with one particular friend. There had to be a connection and he would dig it out.

"Does she fancy her?"

Finch cut in on his partner's wavelength and Wren couldn't resist a quick joke.

"Who? Hannah?"

The reply he got was only for them to know!!

"Don't think it's like that, more control I thought." Wren was serious now. "Or she's just lonely because nobody else gives her a second look."

"That is just the reply you'd expect from a physical point of view. You aren't forgetting the spirit side are you?"

If Wren could have given him a dirty look, it would have said everything but the vibes were there.

"It's that factor that bothers me. And why is Pixel on the scene again?"

"Hmm. I've been wondering that too." Finch was turning something over in his thoughts. "Haven't we noticed before that he seems to come into the act when it is gathering momentum, but that's hardly the case now is it?"

Then his mood changed as though a light had come on.

"Minute."

This meant he was observing something from afar and didn't want any interruption of the wave patterns. His partner remained perfectly still so as not to disturb anything. He let Finch speak first.

"I could be right."

"Explain."

Finch, had he been in body would have taken a deep breath.

"We agree Kieran likes to lay low for periods when he is on a task."

Wren jumped. "You don't mean he is shadowing him or controls him?"

The answer put another twist on things.

"Or is him."

There was an extremely long pause after this as they turned the idea over. Finch could be wrong and going off on a whim, but he wasn't that sort. Wren, from experience had learned never to be surprised at anything although this did put a new slant on things, if it were true.

They did the equivalent of a rewind to see if the two characters had ever been seen at the same time. This was difficult as both could project their image to whatever they chose.

The hierarchy could see through any spiritual disguise but the lesser levels would only see what they were supposed to, rather like a character on stage or in a film could look very different without make up and costume.

"So it's possible that we have been looking at one but thinking we are seeing the other," Wren said.

Finch had to point out one very important fact.

"Yes but both bodily and spiritually. We mustn't forget that. They are very clever illusionists and people will see, or imagine they see what they are meant to."

With these conjectures they knew that nothing could now be taken at face value in any part of this. Although that could sound very confusing, these were highly skilled operators and were sifting through every snippet continually. They would go over an event or conversation many times and suddenly something would hit them that had seemed so innocent before but now had an important bearing as the knowledge built up and the pieces fit together.

Chapter 9

Saturday was always a busy day for Sue and she was glad to get home. Fortunately she didn't have to work on Sundays yet but knew it wouldn't be long before it was put on her rota.

"Your Gran's not happy." Denise told her as she was getting the dinner ready.

"Oh, she had to go back to the hospital today didn't she? Bet that was tough on her."

"Well yes and they gave her a new helper, not very impressed with her. She said to tell you though. High heeled boots, long red fingernails. Ring any bells?"

Sue thought for a moment and said ,"Sounds like a lot I know."

Denise was quiet for a moment then said as casually as she could "Gave her name as Louisa."

"Oh," Sue knew where this was going but still had to put on this outer show because you never knew who had tuned in."

"Yes. Says she likes to be called Lisa."

Sue tried to sound as calm as possible.

"Well there's a lot about, seems to have been a popular name when we were small."

The male members of the family picked up on this but kept their thoughts locked. They must sound normal at all costs. John was glad it was his last shift tonight and Kieran was his not too communicative self and you didn't get much more normal than that. Ask any parent.

Whoever or whatever was on the other side of this game to put it mildly, was a master of strategy. They seemed to know exactly when to do something that would attract interest, then it would seem to die down as though it could appear to have been the onlooker's imagination. This kind of thing in any situation makes one wonder if they have really witnessed something or their mind was playing tricks. Nobody ever wants to look like a fool, so people keep quiet, and that doesn't only apply to the physical state, that is to say that you don't have to be in body at the time, but you don't want any element to think you are going a bit doolally.

So did the higher levels really witness the dust whirls? Had the dust actually been sent to Earth yet? If these were mind games the evil were using, one had to admit they were working.

But as Wren and Finch agreed from past experience, what better way to put one off the scent than to let them believe just that, then when the proverbial back is turned, bang, you hit them and it doesn't matter how many time the phrases 'well I thought it was strange' or I guessed as much' are used, by then it is too late.

It was also noted by the very high levels something that was all too common. You think you have just about sorted what is going on then you are back to square one. It happens all the time but you have to retain what you already know as it can be part of the bigger picture.

One thing now seemed a certainty. The family were not one entity. The three may be but Kieran was not as he was now distancing himself from the others quite a bit, spending most of his home time in his room, still concentrating on the Mars projects. But it had to be remembered, he was still on their wavelength and was privy to every emotion, every thought and even to any plans they may have to make. Strangely the three hadn't seemed to realise this yet and probably thought he was acting his part to perfection.

Wren was sharing his thoughts with Finch.

"This is an experienced group, they would have sussed him out if he had been a 'passenger'."

After a moment Finch added to that.

"Unless, this is also part of their itinerary."

"Which is why they aren't questioning it?" Wren still wasn't convinced. "Are you saying that the three are a cell, but have an extra one tagged on, or they are all part of the same and following instructions?"

Finch gave the impression of a spiritual shrug.

"If we knew that it may answer a lot of questions, but we aren't supposed to, are we or we would have been advised accordingly."

"You always sound like a text book." Wren said with humour. "And you do it when you don't want to answer."

No answer was required but Wren could feel the smugness.

"Got any painkillers?"

Kieran appeared in the lounge where Denise was watching the television at the same time as doing the ironing.

"You got headaches again?" She went to the cupboard and got him a couple.

"Ta". He picked up the tablets. "Is that all I get? I might need some more later."

Denise had only given him two on purpose because she wanted to monitor how many he was taking.

"Then you'll have to ask me again won't you."

He snorted as he went back upstairs but she called after him "They can be addictive and you spend too much time in front of that…" Before she could say 'screen' his bedroom door slammed.

Sue came in from the kitchen.

"What did lazy sod want?"

"Painkillers."

"Did you give him the whole packet? I would have."

Denise had to reprimand her for appearances but it was all for show and then asked "Um, are you going to ring Lisa and ask if it was her at the hospital?"

"Don't know. Can't be arsed. Anyway that's probably what she's expecting."

"She's expecting?" Denise shrilled.

"Mam!" Sue had to laugh. "You're getting as bad as Gran."

"Why, what have I said now?"

"You just don't listen."

After a while Denise was still prodding at the subject.

"So you don't want to know?"

"Know what?" Sue's eyes stayed on the tv.

"And you talk about me!" Denise felt she had put one over on her. "About phoning her. To find out what's going on."

"Aha, that's why you want me to ring. You want to know!"

"Well.. I mean...." Denise was a bit stuck for an excuse "..it's only natural to be interested."

There was a big sigh as Sue reached for her mobile.

"Ok. Ok. I'll put you out of your misery." She pressed the name and waited.

"Hello."

"Hi Lisa. My Mam wants to know if it's you's got the job where my Gran works."

Denise was waving her hand at the way she had put it but her daughter equally waved her down but gave her a nod and a thumbs up.

"Well?" She couldn't wait to ask as the call ended.

Sue shrugged.

"Well nothing much, Yes it's her. Seems she had to take anything or they'd have cut her money off."

"The social?"

"Must be. I didn't want to get too involved or she'd have got clingy again. She treats me like shit."

"Well, you do let her have the upper hand."

Denise was well aware of the game Sue played with her but that too had to be kept on low key. But then she said "You don't mean she's getting a wage?"

"Don't see how she can, it's all voluntary there. So she was saying that for effect. Wonder what the witch is up to."

Denise switched off the iron.

"Well I'd have something to say if me Mam was flogging herself for nothing while that floosie got paid."

"We have another name for that sort now." Sue laughed

"Well I don't want to know what it is." Denise already knew but kept up the façade.

They were right to be cautious for every interchange was being monitored. Wren and Finch were aware of this and it confirmed the fact that there was a reason for interest to be taken in this family. It could be all of them or someone was concentrating on one or even two members. With every aspect it was essential to look at all the alternatives because one missed thing could bring about the downfall of any operation.

Hannah was feeling a bit strange. She didn't know why but something wasn't right. As she got into bed she realised that she couldn't get this Lisa person out of her mind. Hope had noticed this since the first introduction that morning and it wasn't just Hannah feeling put out and not comfortable, there was more to it than that. Also Hope recognised something very familiar about Pixel who was hovering but she couldn't work out what it was. She had also been aware that he had been monitoring Fred which seemed strange. If he was there as Lisa's guardian, why should he take an interest in someone who didn't seem to be very spiritually aware? She wished she could remember where she had come across him before but for now it eluded her.

Fred hadn't been aware of Pixel but his own guardian had been on the scene protecting him constantly and he too was wondering as to the interest. Sometimes spirits, not wanting to be recognised, would use others for a while then release them and although this man had recently been used by the good angels to protect Hannah, he was just as likely a target for evil. For this reason his guardian now called for back up to be on hand should they be required. It wasn't practical to have them too near obviously, but they were in a holding area that was used by many so that individuals couldn't be easily picked out or their subjects noted.

The good angels were also eager to locate the source of the scruffy man/female that hadn't been seen again, at least not in that form. There was also another possibility. Visiting spirits are not supposed to be seen but can often be noticed leaving a room. So could this have been a slip up? The female, which had been confirmed, using this image was seen by Hannah and possibly more. A bit sloppy if this is what happened. But was this yet another distraction? Maybe even nothing and just a chance sighting but if it was a false image there was the possibility it would always be a mystery. We are back to the actor discarding a costume when a play has finished its run.

Sunday promised to be a fairly quiet day for all concerned. John had finished his shift and was ready for bed. Denise would like to have taken the vacuum round but not while he was asleep but there were plenty more jobs to do including preparing dinner, then she intended to put her feet up and just chill for the rest of the day. Hannah was to come round for tea but that was nothing out of the ordinary so she hadn't got to do anything special. Sue had said she intended to have a 'me' day and pamper herself with a hair colour and a new nail polish. Kieran didn't even come into the picture as he would no doubt be locked away except for meals. Even then he expected to be able to take his up to his room but Denise put her foot down and insisted they all eat together on one day at least.

Lisa had plans of her own with or without Pixel's approval.

Even the spirits seemed quiet, but that was far from the truth. Unbeknown to many, there was great activity concerning the Mars situation and trusted scouts were everywhere trying to find the identity of the dispatchers, receivers and possibly heralds. Earth was being continually scanned for the slightest traces of dust but nothing seemed to be detected.

This in itself bothered Wren and Finch who knew the tactics of some of the evil cells. Not only may there be nothing at the moment but it had been known for things to be planted ready for use but so well camouflaged even the high levels couldn't find them. Therefore the dust could have already been planted be well hidden until triggered. An alert went out to all sectors especially the earth spirits who would search way into the crust and even the mantle. The air ones were on particular alert as the dust would have to pass through their sectors to reach earth. Even water spirits had every drop under watch, even to the bottom of the oceans. So all appeared to be covered.

Finch had come up with a possibility and requested audience from above. He and Wren put the idea in front of them.

"Let us just suppose," Finch began "that the dust was transported in a different form."

Wren continued "And then reformed, or assembled back into its original state when it got to its destination."

There was a hush in the surroundings for a moment before the reply came.

"So it wouldn't be detected in transit, and we wouldn't think it necessary to look on earth…because we wouldn't think it was there."

This theory was cause for concern because it was more than possibly the truth and while they were all waiting around for something to happen, not only might it already be there but being added to thus making a very big dangerous evil cell. Even one that could wipe out all the good in its path until it was in complete control of Earth and what else?

"The Moon." Finch suddenly offered. "Have we examined the moon recently? It could be a holding zone."

"But wouldn't that turn red too?" Wren asked.

The hierarchy explained that it would take a long time for it to be noticed from Earth if it were placed on the side facing it. But it could all be put on the far side so that only a probe would pick it up and if the technicians noticed it they wouldn't recognise it for what it was, or may not even see it if it was finely spread."

There was enough doubt to put it under scrutiny so to avoid any suspicion, The Team was made aware.

Wren and Finch returned to their area assured that they would know immediately if anything was found.

It was too quiet. There was a stillness on certain parts of the earth that was uncanny, almost as though something was going to happen. Many thought they were in for a storm but some of the old timers said it wasn't like that, and they should know because they were the best weather forecasters. They could look to the heavens at night and tell you what to expect the next day.

But it didn't stop there. There was something strange in areas of the spirit world that coincided with the earthly locations. This put everyone on full alert. On looking back Finch suddenly hit on something.

"I've just noticed. Whenever we seem to take a step forward, something happens, either to halt us or throw us in another direction."

Wren was silent at first then said "Do you know, I think you're right. Little things that we'd hardly have noticed and…it's when we've been in conference upstairs."

This was worrying. Although thoughts can be monitored, the upper levels have ways of blocking, but that cannot be explained here.

Finch was worried and thought “So when we have returned and mulled over the facts, someone has homed into us.”

They were both quiet as another factor reared its ugly head.

“Or it’s someone up there.” Wren hesitated to even think it.

That was a terrifying thought but had to be considered.

Finch was churning everything over.

“But think about it, it doesn’t have to be one of ours, they could have been intercepted.”

This was even worse.

Short explanation needed with an attempt to keep it as simple as possible.

When the likes of Wren and Finch converse with higher levels they don’t meet up, shake hands and say how good it is to see them! They have to ascend to a level that is high enough to reach them and they are not looking at a familiar person or face. The high ones come down to this exchange level and you can feel they are in presence and the conversation is merely by thought transference, but not in physical terms. That’s fairly obvious.

So although a high one may appear familiar and you think you are conversing with the same one as last time, it may not be the case. Although not a good comparison, if someone phoned you and impersonated someone else voice, you could believe it was that person. So thinking along those lines, the ‘lads’ could have been discussing the situation with an interloper and not of the good variety. Let that sink in for a moment.

As the two recapped their last communication they both hit on the idea to have the moon examined immediately.

“Wait!” Finch stopped. “That could be just what they intended, to take our attention there.”

“And while we are doing that…” Wren didn’t need to finish but added “may not be a bad idea if we could get a volunteer.”

“And leave us free.” Finch was mulling it over.

There were lots of little groups who were used to go and do a bit of snooping, who knew they didn’t ask questions, just got on with it and reported back.

“We’ll use our favourite but they needn’t be all that covert.” Wren thought.

There was another plus side to this. While the snoop team were making it clear they were searching for something, they would definitely be under scrutiny, so they could make a meal of it. They would be given the gist of the plan, but would still act as though they didn’t want to be noticed.

Without hesitation it was put into action immediately without prior notification to any high levels.

“Now we will see.” The two agreed.

The family also noticed the change in atmosphere and were concerned about it. Each of them had witnessed this sort of thing before and it didn’t bode well.

Hannah was round for tea and she too seemed rather quiet.

“Bet you’re tired after going back.” Denise was referring to the coffee shop.

“Hmm, oh yes a bit. Very ummm, exacting.” Hannah didn’t quite know how to put it.

“Oh you mean with the new girl?”

“Well, that wasn’t the umm, best thing.”

She wasn’t being very explicit but it was obvious she had taken a dislike to her.

“Well I don’t think she’ll last long by what you’ve said.”

“Depends, doesn’t it?”

Denise looked at her.

“On what?”

Hannah did one of her looks and shrugged.

“It depends on who she is, well you know …with.”

“You’ll have to explain Mam, you’re loosing me.” Denise had a very good idea what her mother was on about but wanted her to voice it.

Hannah leant over and whispered.

“You know, in with the boss and that sort of thing.”

This was followed by a nod and a very knowing look.

“Oh I doubt that.”

“Well we’ll see won’t we?”

At that point Kieran came into the room.

"See what?"

"None of your business you nosey little beggar." John joined in now.

Kieran pulled a face went into the kitchen and gave a V sign to the door.

"And show some respect to your elders." John's voice came from the lounge.

Sue had been listening to this quietly but then said "Don't worry Gran, there's a way of getting rid of people you know."

"What?" Hannah looked shocked.

"Oh we get them at work, the slackers, but they don't last long."

"Why dear? What do you do?"

Sue smiled. "Oh we don't need to do anything, but they just go."

"Well I'm lost." Hannah said.

Kieran reappeared and went straight through to go back to his room.

"Are you coming back down?" Denise called after him but was met with silence.

"We wouldn't have been allowed to do that." Hannah said.

"What's that Gran?"

"Not answer for one thing and not sit with the family."

Sue said kindly, "But things have changed a lot, we don't all sit round and play parlour games you know, we do our own thing."

Hannah was quiet for a moment then almost whispered, "No respect that's what it is."

If ever a family could have appeared normal, they didn't come any better than this bunch.

As soon as Hannah had been taken home, it was time to try and work out what was going on in the surroundings. All the family members were too experienced to be open even in their thoughts but odd remarks flitted in an instance. They knew something was in the offing, but when and where? It had been like it all day and the waiting could get to the impatient ones but these knew better.

It could well be nothing to do with them but a ripple from something near or far depending on how big the occurrence was. Instinct was telling them it was building for something yet to happen so they had to be on the alert but hide it.

Sue's phone rang.

"Oh it's her." She pulled a face.

"Well answer it?" Denise was pointing at it.

Sue pressed the button "Yes?"

"Oh Hi. Look why not pop round for a bit?"

"Well I'm a bit busy."

"The hell you are. Playing happy families?" She laughed.

"I was talking to me Mam."

"Well, I'm sure we've got more interesting things to talk about."

"No really, I…"

"Good see you soon." And the call was finished.

Sue almost threw the mobile on the chair.

"Going?" Was all Denise asked with a knowing look.

"Lion's den."

"Hmm."

"I don't want to but…"

"You know you have to so get it over with."

There was more in that exchange than the onlooker would perceive. Jobs had to be done and this was one that couldn't be put off.

It was just unfortunate that all the vibes were wrong, and they knew it.

Sue had tried to act the simple girl with Lisa which had worked for a while, but she knew she had to up her game as the other one was plotting something. She stood at the door and tapped lightly. It was opened almost immediately which was unusual as Lisa liked to keep people waiting, as a form of control which was what she was all about.

"Oh." Sue jumped on purpose.

"Knew you'd come you see." The tone was sarcastic.

"Can't stay long, got to get things ready for tomorrow."

"Oh you worry too much. Let life flow over your, I do." Lisa let the way into the lounge. "Sorry about the mess."

"Mess?" Sue looked round. It was tidier than she'd ever seen it.

"Well, you never know do you?" The eyes went up.

Anyone else would have felt very uneasy but Sue was used to this kind of tactic and Lisa was up to something.

They were sitting drinking coffee and Lisa turned the conversation round to her job but Sue was only half listening because, as Essie she was trying not to notice Pixel's presence.

"But it will do until I hotch her out."

"Sorry, hotch who out?"

"The old dear. Doesn't need two of us and well, she's a bit past it isn't she?"

It was time for action. Sue was going in for the kill.

"Well, Louisa, sorry Lisa, not only do you know very well who that is but also I was very surprised to hear you were able to even set foot in the place."

"What the hell you on about?" Lisa's looked changed rapidly.

"Well you must be grieving. In case you'd forgotten didn't one of your relatives die in that fire?"

"I – I- well actually, no."

Sue tipped her head on one side showing she was expecting a barrage of lies but she kept silent forcing the other one to confess.

"It wasn't. We were told wrong. Terrible shock though as you can imagine."

"Keep babbling." Sue thought as she gave a very sarcastic knowing smile but kept silent letting the other one put herself into a corner.

Lisa seemed to be running out of words trying to explain the first shock then the relief.

"But you see," Sue was smirking now "that doesn't exactly add up does it?"

"Look does it matter? It turned out ok in the end so what's your beef?"

A pause for effect.

"Well I wouldn't say that to Janice's family, I don't think they would think it had 'turned out ok in the end." She repeated the words for effect.

Lisa knew she was being dangled.

"Look what's your game?" She almost shouted and Pixel moved to calm her.

"Me? Game? Oh I don't think I'm the one playing a game but I will tell you one thing. If even one hair of my Gran's head is hurt, you'd better start running, but you will never have a place to hide."

With that she got up, went to the door, turned and repeated "even one hair." And she was gone.

"Well that didn't go as you expected." Pixel smirked as he rubbed the salt in.

"And you did a shitting lot about it!"

He was silent.

"And what's that little cow up to?"

Pixel made himself obvious as he stood in front of Lisa.

"I think you've stirred up the muck, to put it politely."

"She's different." Lisa was fuming as she felt for the first time that Sue had the upper hand, which was just how her 'friend' had planned it.

"Or the same."

"Now what the bloody hell are you on about?"

Pixel gave the impression of a big sigh.

"Oh why do they have to put me guarding such trash, why can't I get the proper ladies?"

"Hmm, you'd feel at home there wouldn't you?" The remark was meant to be cutting and hit home.

He gave her a moment then said "Her guardian isn't like me."

"I don't think anyone is like you sweetheart."

"Will you listen!" His tone brought her down to earth.

"Ok. Ok. Keep your thong on."

When he knew he had her interest he continued.

"Her guardian isn't separate."

"You've lost me." She reached for a drink but he stopped her arm before she could grab the bottle.

"They are one and the same."

"You're talking bollocks."

"Look, we are separate right?" He was right in her face now.

"Thank Christ for that!"

"But they aren't. Don't you see? You aren't dealing with a quiet little mouse here. She is high up. So what's she doing here?"

Now she was listening. She looked at him for he was still visible, then away as if she was thinking, then back.

"She's a witch?"

He was beginning to wish he'd never started this but it was his job to protect her, and in this case she must be warned. For all he knew she could be a target for whatever reason. But it wasn't sinking in.

"No my dear thing, not a witch. A single spirit. Not like us. Now do you get it?"

"Yeah, but I don't know what it means. Hang on, doesn't everyone have a guardian angel thingy. I've had a few."

"Yes and don't we know it?" He kept to himself but answered "That's right. That's what is supposed to happen."

"So why didn't they give her one then?"

He felt very inclined to give Lisa one in a minute and not an angel!

"Look, I know it's unusual so let me make it simple. People like that, who don't need a separate angel are usually out on a task. It could be anything."

"Oh. What sort of task?"

"If we knew that..."

He knew that any amount of explanation would only go to waste so he told her just to be extremely careful of whom she associated with.

He faded from sight leaving her quite bewildered but knew he had to do some investigating of his own to find out more about her friend.

Hope had left a stand-in watching Hannah while she went to observe Pixel from a distance. She had to know where she had seen him before and it seemed a coincidence that he should be guarding Lisa who had turned up to work with Hannah. She now rose to a higher level so she could look down. There he was, hovering around Lisa but sending out vibes that he wasn't at ease. His charge was busy trying out new nail polishes and other items of make up and didn't appear to be in touch with anything other than her earthly self.

Then as his appearance seemed to merge into another identity, Hope had her answer.

Chapter 10

Something new had come into the mix. The Team had been extra vigilant and reported that the grey coloured dust on the moon had been disturbed recently, also on expanding their search, the sands of the Sahara had an extra layer of brown dust in places. This made them check other deserts but no others showed this trace. In such a terrain it is very difficult to keep anything in one place for it to be examined, as the sand is always moving and a sandstorm can destroy any traces of newly deposited dust, and will have spread it over a wider area. Following this they had returned to the moon to check the movement of dust there.

What they found sent ripples through all levels. Wren and Finch were summoned to hear the findings but they kept their thoughts close due to their recent worry about an imposter. This is how it was explained.

"The dust from the moon has been sent to earth as a marker but placed where we wouldn't notice it. The Mars dust then homes in on those places and sends the brown dust which none of us were looking for. We were looking for red." Before anyone could query this the answer was given. "Why brown? Simple. What colour does blood become after a while if it is left on a dressing or a surface? It turns brown, so the brown dust is still the return of the evil bodies."

It confirmed that the red dust was a decoy and only sent to draw the good forces away from the actual operation. It also meant that the brown could have been coming in for a while unnoticed and it would be waiting, maybe until a designated amount was in place or for certain instructions. But there was the fact that it would have to be moved from the desert as it wasn't about to do much harm there surely.

As Wren and Finch returned they knew that whatever the operation was it was now underway.

"Do you think this means they don't need a herald?" Wren wondered. "If the grey sand is already a marker, wouldn't that be enough?"

Finch wasn't certain and said "I don't think we can come to any definite answer yet, and we will continue to churn over what we know."

"All the pieces of the puzzle aren't in play." Wren seemed sure.

Although his partner agreed, it didn't make it any simpler knowing they would have to wait for the evil's next move.

"Unless," Finch jumped "they are forced."

"How?" Wren didn't see how they could engineer any change.

"No, but there may be those who can."

"Oh, and I suppose you have a list?" Although it was said with humour Wren was well aware of the level of danger they were dealing with.

After a moment Finch expressed the thought that it may be time to play them at their own game and use some of the evil. Throw them a few red herrings. Let them be the players on the front line and just stand back and watch.

Wren wasn't too sure about this and wished his friend was a bit more specific but at this stage you couldn't take any chances. Any thoughts could be tapped so they had to be squashed immediately.

By rights any plans had to be passed by the next levels above, you couldn't just go about doing your own thing and then if you got into problems expect the higher ones to pull you out. However in this instance caution was needed so the lads would have to tread carefully but not leave any tracks.

It was becoming clear that Pixel was using Lisa as a tool to get to Sue. He wasn't one to go in directly but always laid a confusing trail Hope now knew things would not go smoothly due to events that had gone on in the past and kept reappearing in different scenarios. Also she knew that Hannah would be drawn into this.

Although Sue had kept her image close, she had been aware of someone guarding Lisa and knew he had identified her by her single spirit. Until then she had no idea it was Pixel or of his close connection due to his false image but there are always little give aways. When you have been in close contact with someone, there are things you pick up but think nothing of and eventually when they slip for a moment, you remember. It can be a glance, a word or even just a feeling. Had she been there in spirit with Hope she would have identified him when he slipped back into his normal appearance. However as she neared home something stirred in her psychic memory and she now knew who was in the area. In seconds she and Hope were in conference for they knew something was being planned and with Pixel it wouldn't be good.

As Sue walked back into her home she knew the kind of reception she was going to get. Obviously the other family members picked up on her recent revelation but had to keep it under very low key.

"How was your friend?" Denise tried to make it sound as natural as possible.

"Well, I don't think she'll hack it for long." Sue gave a false laugh.

"I wondered how long she'd cope with getting her hands dirty."

"She's not right for it is she?"

"Who's not right for it?" Kieran was doing one of his passing through moments and of course was well aware of the exchange.

"Mind your business." His mother snapped. "As my Gran would have said 'you want to know the ins and outs of Meg's arse'."

Although she'd used it many times it always seemed to come out funny.

"Well you can shove it up your arse." He retaliated.

It didn't matter how much Denise shouted after him he was already in the kitchen.

"Take no notice of him Mam, he only does it to look big."

John joined in for good measure.

"If my dad had spoken his mother like that, Granddad would have taken his belt to him."

If any passers by had be homing in on this exchange they would have taken it as a normal family conversation and moved on by now. So the four now updated on Sue's recent findings. They dare not dwell on it but it was locked in their memory banks.

Wren and Finch, having also witnessed the exchange were now sure that this family unit were working together for the first time. They had obviously been selected due to them all being 'at one' with their spirit. But the history of Sue and Pixel and also Hope had still to be revealed, as the knowledge was being squashed for the time being for fear of putting anyone at further risk.

But Finch was pretty sure they had identified one character. The scruffy man/female.

Wren was weighing it up.

"You know Pixel, comes over as very effeminate. I mean it could be an act but it seems so natural somehow."

"Yes he flits between both sexes. Or hovers in the middle however the mood takes him or the job demands." It didn't come as any surprise to Finch as he'd come across these characters before.

"So he's both." Wren finished it.

"I think he appears as either but his main leaning is to the feminine, that's why when he tried to appear as a scruffy bloke…"

"It was picked up as a female!" Wren almost announced. "And then Lisa gets the job in the shop."

"Sadly after Janice went."

They were silent for a moment almost out of respect but then two things came to the fore.

One. They still couldn't be positive that Hannah was the actual target.

Two. Now Janice had rested, they could communicate with her in spirit.

Pixel had a score to settle. In a previous life he and Sue had planned to marry but he had treated her so disrespectfully she called it off. This made him look a fool but also brought to light that he was not the nice person he portrayed. He vowed to get even with her one day however long it took. He had come back in a following life as a woman and tried to get her into another relationship and again she had rejected him. By now his anger was taking over and he turned for assistance to powers you should never use. But evil is always ready to take on new members and before he knew it he was having to carry out their orders. Oh yes he would get what he wanted, but there is always a price. And this would take an eternity to be paid but that meant there was no end.

Now he was promised that he would get even with her at last but he would have to do it their way. They even controlled his sexual image which is why they had him swapping from one to the other as it suited them. But the major task was not Sue. She was what they used to control him. Although the evil didn't know why she was here or if she was on a task, it didn't matter, she just had to be within his grasp and they must keep that going until the main operation was finished. Then nothing would matter.

Having delved into the past history Wren and Finch had an idea that Pixel was being used but they couldn't be certain for what. At the moment they couldn't be sure if he was involved in the Mars issue, and he may have nothing to do with it, but the door was always open to any latest information. After all the family were still a mystery and their presence at this moment in time could be more than just coincidence.

The Team had detected another grey deposit followed quickly by a brown one, again in the Sahara. Somehow the good forces had expected the brown to be scattered around the globe not just centred in one area but time would tell. This may be a tester or part of a larger pattern. The problem was that they couldn't scrape it up and send it back. It would have to remain where it was for now, or would it? A message was left for The Team to ask if the new dust could be dispatched back in any way. The answer surprised even the hierarchy.

"Job done."

As the news filtered down, Finch was rather thoughtful and his partner wanted to know why.

"Think about it." Finch was very serious. "We don't know anything about The Team apart from there is supposed to be such an element. We know how to request help but that changes constantly. Now think. When have you ever heard of an instant reply?"

"Well, I don't think we have." Wren was feeling worried.

"So why one now?" He waited for the obvious answer.

"To throw us off the scent."

They were deep in concentration for several moments. This meant that maybe The Team had gone in but who was it that had replied?

Immediately the message was sent to the higher levels who were already on this wavelength. It was impossible for this select force to have been infiltrated because no one at all were certain of who they were, how they acted or anything about them. Often they didn't have to be summoned, they just knew help was needed. It was often thought they were homing in on all the higher angel communications. So how had anyone managed to reply for them? The only other explanation was that they had actually sent the message but no one was convinced of that.

As people were starting to take holidays before the rush, Hannah had been asked to go in for a few hours every day until further notice. This pleased her as she liked to be busy, but the idea of working with 'that girl' as she called Lisa wasn't such a pleasant thought. She knew she wasn't suitable the moment they were introduced but couldn't do anything about it. They'd had a variety of people come and go and she hoped this one would be in the 'go' category.

This did give Hope the chance of keeping a close eye on her and Pixel as he would be hovering, probably in his latest image, but he must have recognised her already. She thought back to Lisa's first day and knew that Pixel must have spotted her then but had given no sign of it. There again, he wouldn't would he? If he was trying to go under the radar he would have to ignore anyone who might recognise him. So in a way she was one up by having seen him shed his fake image, but obviously he didn't know that.

She also realised that he had wanted people to think that it was Lisa that was after Sue, whereas he was simply using her for his own purposes. She was no more than a dummy. As Hope started putting all the pieces together she was looking at a different plot which would require new tactics. But for now she must guard Hannah because in a way she was also in the firing line being a connection, so caution must be used for her safety.

Kieran had been busy. Everyone accepted that being a teenager he would be offhanded, often rude and prefer his company to that of the family so he was able to loose himself in his room without question. The other three guessed there was more to it than that but did not interfere. When groups such as this are formed they can be working together or can all be on totally different missions. They put on a face for all to see, but then carry on with their orders without question. In this case it was vital for him to have plenty of space and time without having to interact with anyone. Also a character can be included just to make up the numbers. So any one of the family could be an innocent bystander and just be there without any specific purpose. The one thing you didn't do was ask questions. For one thing it could ruin a whole or maybe several operations and the rule in general was you didn't do it.

More often than not, while Kieran was lying on his bed, Kane was far away for his task was not in the immediate vicinity. He had picked up the thought that he may be Pixel which could be useful. Spirits often use other images to throw the scent and he could let people believe he was in one place whereas he could be on the other side of the solar system.

At the moment even Wren and Finch were oblivious of his activities so this was not a lowly spirit but a highly trained operative, but on which side? There was the possibility that he could be a receiver or decoy and had placed the red dust at his father's works but no one had reason to even consider that. For now he was almost invisible which was just how he had to be.

John was between shifts and had a day off so he offered to take Hannah to work, an offer she gratefully accepted. But he did have an ulterior motive.

"It's our Denise's birthday soon and as usual I haven't got a clue as to what she wants. Any ideas?" He said as they made their way to the hospital.

"Well, you know what would be nice. She's always looking after you lot, so why don't you take her for a nice meal? Give her a night off."

He was quiet for a moment. "You think she'd really go for that? I mean it's not a present is it?"

Hannah smiled. "You know they call me old fashioned but you're no better. It's what they do these days. They go out. Let someone else do the cooking and the washing up. And as for something to look at, well let me tell you they soon become dust collectors."

"Well if you really think she'd go a bundle on it?"

"Trust me. She'll love it. And the kids are old enough to take care of themselves. Probably stuff themselves with that junk food we were on about."

"Well, that's certainly a thought. Thanks." John pulled up and she got out.

She smiled as she made her way inside.

"Wouldn't mind a nice man taking me out once in a while." She mused.

As she was on the early shift she walked up just as Fred was unlocking the shutters.

"Morning m'dear. He smiled. "You look happy. What you been up to?"

"Oh nothing, was just telling that son in law of mine to take our Denise out for a meal for her birthday."

"And is he?"

Denise took off her coat. "Not sure. Funny lot kids aren't they?"

"That's strange. You stand back." Fred ordered. "Something's leaked, look. I'll get a mop then see where it's come from. Don't step on it. Don't know what it is yet."

As Hannah stood there looking at the floor she had a strange feeling as though someone was trying to get her attention. Hope was at her side holding her back for this wasn't right. There was nothing around that could have leaked or spilled.

Fred returned and warned her again to keep back. He gingerly touched the floor with his mop then looked closely. It wasn't sticky, it wasn't water, in fact he didn't know what it was but thought he'd better mop it up anyway.

"Wait a minute." Hannah was being prompted by Hope. "I think I know what that is. Can I have a paper towel please?"

She bent down and dabbed the towel on the stuff and smelled it.

"Well?" Fred asked.

Hope was prompting again.

"I might be wrong but I think it's that stuff that we used to clean the cold drinks machine with."

"Well what's it doing here on the floor?" He looked again. "And it's not been there long and it was all shut up yesterday. Can't have been here since Saturday."

"But we don't use that machine now. They took it out when…when the place had to be done." She didn't like to mention the fire.

Hope wasn't happy with this. It was almost as though someone or something, had put it there knowing she would be the first in after Fred had rolled up the shutter, and not seeing it she would have slipped.

All this was noted by Wren and Finch who still felt Hannah was at risk although why, was still a mystery.

This may be a good time to explain Pixel's mirrors as they are called. Several spirits have mastered this art and while we pause at the coffee shop for a moment it could explain something.

Imagine you are in a place and you want to contact someone else, also there but you can't see them. If mirrors are placed at the right angles you can see round corners for example, and with many mirrors you could cover say a whole building. Sounds simple in earthly terms but think of this in the spiritual. When Hannah saw the scruffy man, even just his image, he didn't have to be anywhere near. He could have been mirroring.

But, you may ask, how would he know who was going to see the image with so many people about? You are thinking physical. The answer obviously is that this is a spiritual talent and the sender would select their subject then 'send' the image to them only, unless of course they intended it to be seen by many.

So now it has to be realised that Hannah was targeted for whatever reason. Keeping an open mind Pixel could have been there to warn her, but if that were the case, why did she also then get the warning from the apparently old lady?

It was clear that if Hannah was still a target, the protection must be upped immediately.

Denise had been ticking along as the mother of the family hardly noticed for anything other than her outward self, but like Kieran she could be using her body for one thing but simultaneously be far away on a job as Dee not recognisable, for she could take on any identity to suit the matter in hand. In fact all those with no extra guardian had the same talent but on different levels of experience. Sue was lower than these two and John was even lower than that but nevertheless both very adept in using what skill they had. They never worked together in spirit as that could have filtered into their physical persona, so each one was there now for a totally different purpose.

That cleared up one question for Wren and Finch, this was not a group operation. In some ways it could sound better but it opened up the fact that there would be four different tasks being undertaken and all could be leading to the same end but also may have no connection at all. This pair always wished they had a bit of inside information in cases such as these, but it could never been like that for many operatives were under secret orders which could be wiped from their spiritual memories in an instance if danger threatened.

It did create another query though. They may be on different assignments but were they all working on the same side? It had occurred a few times before to their knowledge, that the members accepted they didn't ask questions from the others and had been working from both the good and evil sides, so were in fact fighting each other and wondering why they weren't getting results. This was something that would have to be watched closely without being detected, because at this point neither Wren nor Finch had any inkling of who was batting for whom.

They looked at them as individuals now. Dee would just disappear without trace as did Kane. It was suspected that Sue as Essie was placed as a bait to bring Pixel down for good as he was not appearing to be a very wholesome character and there was much more to him than was immediately obvious. John seemed to be a spare part at the moment. He had been used to see the red dust, even with the disastrous consequences, but anyone could have done that. If he was on a mission, it was yet to be recognised.

Hannah looked at the rota. She thought there was supposed to be another lady helping for a couple of hours during the morning but nobody was listed and Lisa wasn't due to come on until midday.

Fred checked back with her to make sure there had been no other spillage of any kind but she assured him everything was in order.

"Don't think I'll put it in the book," he whispered "not as if it was anything hazardous and you haven't slipped on it."

"No, they'll either ignore it completely or make a meal out of it." Hannah agreed.

Sometimes it was better to keep quiet than let someone score 'brownie points' for being over zealous, and there were always those struggling to climb the ladder by whatever means.

A man from admin then appeared with a woman in tow. It seemed the original one couldn't come so they had taken on the next one in the queue. She was introduced, but funnily enough as soon as her name had been given, Hannah had forgotten it.

"Must be getting forgetful." She thought. It wasn't like her, as she'd always been good with names.

But this time it was not that. She wasn't supposed to remember it.

"I'm sorry, I didn't catch your name." She smiled.

"Oh didn't you?" Was the short reply.

"Would you mind telling...?"

"It's one of those that you can never pronounce so don't worry about it."

"Well I have to call you something." Hannah was insistent as she was being prodded to pursue this by Hope.

"Get her name. Get her name." Was being pushed into her brain.

"I'll write it down for you, later."

There seemed to be nothing else she could do so Hannah showed her what her job would be and took her own position at the till.

Hope knew who this was and was determined to put her under pressure. It was a great disguise but she wondered how long it would be before Hannah suspected it. Unfortunately Hope knew she would have been recognised so couldn't do anything to change her own image but all she could do was not let the woman realise she had been identified at that point.

"So, you are only here for two hours ummm...". Hannah went as if to say a name but it wasn't going to work.

"All I can do. But they are glad of anyone by the looks of it."

This was a bit rude, but Hannah decided that for the short time it would be, she would keep quiet.

"Of course I usually handle the money." The woman added.

Before she could stop herself Hannah, with Hope's intervention answered, "Well you don't here."

"Oh, so you don't trust anyone?"

Hannah turned and looked at her.

"Most people come here to offer their services. We do whatever job we are given and those of us who have been here the longest do the till."

"Well, if it keeps you happy."

Hope was watching closely and thought "Patronising bitch!"

She tried to put as much doubt in Hannah's mind as possible and then resumed trying to find out what this person was doing here but there was something she had to check on first.

Requesting a temporary stand in she then visited Denise's workplace but she was not at her desk. Doing a quick scan of the place she found her lying on a bed in the medical room. She had come over dizzy and needed time to feel well enough to return to her work, but in fact she needed to leave Denise for a short while and work as Dee. It was obvious that in this state she could also act in the physical form so she was certainly of high level.

Short explanation. Some single entities can move around spiritually whilst leaving their body to do its normal things therefore drawing no attention to themselves. But the higher ones can shut down their body and put it in a state of rest but then take on their other identity using a bodily form. This was what Denise was doing now.

It was suspected that the very very high levels could use two bodies simultaneously but it was quite rare.

Hope had her answer and returned to take over with Hannah. It was obvious Dee wasn't there to protect her earth mother and equally certain that she was more than aware of Hope leaving for a moment and then returning.

"Let's see what she does about this." The thought was in Hope's being for a millisecond.

"Hello, you new?" Fred's voice cut into the situation.

Dee was distracted for a moment.

"Me, oh yes, just for a while."

He would never know why he answered what he did but the words were formed for him.

"Thought you were a patient."

"Oh why?" She would rather not have got into conversation about herself.

"You look familiar, that's all."

"Well you must see lots of people and they all look alike after a while I expect."

"Oh, I never forget a face." Fred looked straight at her then walked off, but turned and looked over his shoulder.

Hope had used him well and she knew this had rankled Dee as she wasn't used to being recognised and any suggestion of it was unwelcome. Hannah of course was oblivious to all this going on and was more concerned over the attitude of this new woman. What with her, and then Lisa coming in at twelve, it wasn't going to be one of the best days she could tell.

Dee had known that Hope would be in the area but had expected to have achieved more than she did. It was obvious this guardian wasn't going to let anyone get at her charge which would seem they both had to be on the same side so there would be two to tackle when the time came. But she had learned one important thing. Neither of them were that high up so they shouldn't be too much of a problem. She knew Hope would recognise her spiritually, but you didn't have to be that clever to spot someone and there was no need at this stage to go in for any dramatic cover up. But Hope may have to be removed for a while when she went in to execute her eventual assignment.

How Hannah got through the next couple of hours she would never know, and twelve o'clock couldn't come quick enough.

"Will you be coming again?" She asked the woman thinking 'please say no'.

"Well I wouldn't think so, but there again you never know do you?"

At first Hannah's heart jumped for joy but then dropped.

"Oh well. Thank you for your help. Good bye."

The brush off couldn't have been clearer and she hoped she had made the point that she wouldn't be welcome.

As Dee returned to be Denise, she felt smug.

"Should be a push over. You don't know what's going to hit you madam."

Chapter 11

What any onlooker didn't know was that Dee hadn't come of her own free will, she had been summoned. Although she was sending out false vibes of who could be on whose side, it was a common practice to throw any eavesdroppers off the scent. Most of the time this kind of operator rarely let the true facts even enter the area, so they were existing in a false world, again like the actor on the stage. But with some the stage was almost a permanent state.

In the short time Hope was checking on Denise's physical whereabouts, Dee and Hannah had communicated. But the question Wren was now asking was "Had Hope actually set a trap, forcing their hands?"

Finch was trying to piece the information together because this had thrown a new light on things.

"So innocent little Hannah was not what she appeared to be."

"Well she's covered it well." Wren added. "Up to now she has played no part in it, just been there to give birth to Denise."

"And act the insignificant little granny."

After a moment's cogitation Finch was trying to put everything in perspective, but somehow he couldn't make sense of it.

"So if Dee was summoned it had to be by Hannah. But why, if she was herself already there as this person with no name?"

"Because they couldn't communicate on the physical level, it would have made too many ripples in the surrounding atmosphere." Wren answered.

"Right. And they would have had to wait until Hope was out of the way, but what if she hadn't gone?"

"Unless they set the trap." Wren stopped. "They knew that if she suspected who this new helper was, she would have to go and check on Denise."

“You’re thinking along my lines.” Finch agreed. “It was all arranged. So Hannah needed to communicate with Dee but not in the family setting. So what was so important to bring her out of the woodwork?”

“But we thought we had checked her out long ago.” Wren was pondering not wanting to admit they had let someone slip through the net.

“One big question.” Finch was brief and to the point. “Just how big is she?”

“To be able to summon one as high as Dee, pretty high I’d say.”

“Or,” Finch thought “just a messenger.”

“Would Dee jump as quickly to ‘just a messenger’ as you put it?”

“We don’t know what the set up is, but we do know that they are trying to be as covert as possible.”

Wren wanted another answer.

“And is Hope on the ball?”

“If you mean is she aware of what’s happened, that’s debatable but needs to be monitored but don’t forget the possibility that she possibly set the trap for them to be able to communicate.”

There were too many questions but not enough answers at this point, but that meant they had to be found, and quickly. It still didn’t prove which side anyone was working. Because there were interactions didn’t necessarily make them on the good or bad. This is where holding back was essential as long terms plans had often been ruined by an entity jumping in too soon.

In case anyone has wondered about the security of stand in spirits similar to the one Hope used, there are two options.

One is to have someone equal who will immediately impart any updates on your return, then they go back to their business drawing a line under the knowledge.

The other is to have a slightly lesser spirit, but one still skilled enough to spot intruders, and when they leave, it’s like playing back a recording of what they have witnessed, but they go on their way retaining no knowledge of it.

The upper levels were rather concerned as to the apparent lack of reports regarding the dust, of any colour. There was nothing to confirm any movement and the question arose as to whether they should keep despatching the physical remains to Mars. It was decided to carry on for now but be very observant especially when the deposits were being made. They were instructed to also be extra vigilant when sending the evil spirits to the magenta hole as traps could be laid there and it wouldn't be the bad that were sucked in.

Sue liked to go outside for her lunch if the weather was good enough. She loved working with people but it was nice to switch off for a moment and relax before going back for another session. Her phone rang.

"Now what?" She looked at the screen. "Oh no. Not her." It was Lisa.

"Yes?" She almost snapped.

"I'm going spare here. Your gran is working the nuts off me."

Sue was tempted to remind her she hadn't any nuts but instead said "So what am I supposed to do about it?"

"Well you're always going on about me getting a job."

"I meant a proper job, one that earns money, not voluntary just to give you something to do." Then after a pause "They don't pay you do they?"

"Not as such."

"Oh no. Now what are you up to?" Sue hardly dare ask.

"Well, I get to meet people."

"And that's it is it?" Sue glanced at her watch. This isn't how she'd intended spending her lunch break.

"Well, talent is a bit short but you never know who you will meet do you?"

"Lisa, if you're trying to tell me something, for goodness sake spit it out and stop playing games. I'm due back in."

"Well, if you're interested, I mean it's not for me to say is it. Being family like."

"Look I haven't got time for silly games Lisa. I have to go."

"Ok but when I went in today, the new woman that was leaving gave me a funny look, you know, like she knew me."

"And did she?" Sue sounded exasperated but in fact an alarm bell went off."

"How should I know? I didn't know her, but I got the feeling that when she saw me she left quickly before we could talk, you know what I mean."

"No, I haven't a clue and I'm not particularly interested. Now, unless you have any more useless scraps of information I have to go. Bye."

"Bye. But your gran didn't look too pleased." And the call was ended.

In fact Sue was very interested. She kept her earthly image strong but knew she had to mull over this seemingly bit of trivia as there was more to this than seemed obvious. Also it was though this 'friend' had been instructed to tell her because she was very familiar with the method.

People are often used to impart information without realising. So Lisa thought it was a bit of idle gossip, because she had little else to think about, whereas she had been used. There are times when people say "I don't know why I said that." Of course they don't. It didn't come from them but was channelled because they were in the right place at the right time.

When the time was right and there were no distractions, Sue decided she would try and communicate with Hope without seeming too obvious because you never knew who was eavesdropping. Pixel had to be behind this because of previous encounters and she wanted him out for good. If he was using this little 'tart' he was on a looser.

"The game's hotting up." Wren had been interested in the previous events.

Finch seemed a bit concerned though.

"But something's drawing them out and that is worrying."

"Yes but have you noticed, certain ones are making the moves whilst others are merely watching."

"True but I think they are trying to draw everyone out into the open which is strange in itself."

Wren thought for a moment.

"Yes, the main ploy is always to remain hidden so…." He paused as if piecing it together "they've got to expose some to make them vulnerable."

They both were trying to put all the pieces in the right place but there were too many gaps.

"Ok. Let's boil it down." Finch decided. "Take them one by one and tie in what we know."

"I'm ready." Wren would like to have been first to state the obvious but let his partner list everything.

"Right. At the moment, John seems to be an outside player, even one to just make up the numbers so we'll leave him for now."

"And he seems to be the least experienced." Wren added.

"True, but don't ever let that fool you, it can be a cover." Finch had to add before he continued.

"Denise/Dee seems to have made the first move but we know she was summoned, but was that by Hannah or Hope? Either one would be strange. We didn't think Hannah was of any importance and Hope wouldn't contact her."

"I've been wondering about that from the start." Wren agreed. "And what went on between Dee and Hannah that we missed?"

"Ok. Let's move on." Finch wanted to cover everyone and see who had the most anomalies.

"Sue, well she is aware of Pixel and that will be her main concentration but in so doing it could also cover what her real job is."

"So she would use it for that."

"Kieran. Let's leave him for now. Not playing an active part."

"So now we come to Hannah." Wren said with meaning.

"Yes, Hannah. She has to be in on all this and has hidden well up to now, but she is in danger of being constantly monitored which won't be very good if she has an assignment to put into practice."

"Unless," Wren cut in, "that's exactly what she engineered. She could be a decoy and while she is being watched…"

"…the main plan is carried out elsewhere." Finch finished for him.

After a slight pause Wren asked "And is Hope a main player?"

"She's certainly in the mix somewhere but I don't think she is calling the shots." Then he added "And don't forget the other two. Pixel and his underling, Lisa."

"Do you think there are others that we haven't traced yet?" Wren wondered.

"Not in the main game. I think we have them all in front of us." Finch seemed to be turning something over so Wren knew it was best to let him sort it out before interrupting. He didn't have to wait long.

"Apart from the family situation, which is only a base for them all to use as a cover, to carry out their individual operations, don't forget the dust, and the holes."

"We still don't know what is happening about the black hole disposal idea." Wren thought.

Finch was looking further. "And if the magenta hole or holes are compromised, as we suspected we could be at risk, and maybe the evil will not be permanently destroyed."

These were serious facts and if there was a connection, they had to find it fast or it would be too late.

Pixel was furious. Lisa was asleep, flopped out on the sofa in a most unladylike pose. He needed to use her as time was running out. He knew from old that as soon as Sue knew he was trailing her she would be out of the area, but the only thing that gave him hope was the fact that she could be on a job and was forced to stay until it was completed. But he needed Lisa to be in touch with her and look at her! Useless bit of garbage. He would have to wake her up.

Being asleep her spirit had travelled but of course it was still connected by her light line, so all he had to do was follow it and bring her back to body. Then she could get of her ugly backside and carry out his wishes.

He followed it much further than he expected and considered doing a 'pull'. If someone is needed to return to body immediately, their guardian has to 'pull' them back to consciousness and it can feel like a very strong jerk. This wasn't easy depending on how far away she was and how much she wanted to stay there. But he wasn't the most patient soul so decided to have a go, as he put it. He returned to her body, still in its ungainly pose, and pulled strongly on her line. He wasn't prepared for what happened next.

The opposing tug wrenched him upward at such a speed until he felt he had hit a wall and his grasp had gone. The shock was such that he was disorientated for several moments and it took quite a while before he could return to Lisa's bodily form. She hadn't moved and he noticed her light line was very thin which meant it was stretched to the limits. There was no way he was going to try that again which meant all he could do was wait.

As a guardian he should have been at her side constantly never leaving her spirit, but somehow she, or some other force had fooled him and he had no idea where she was. He couldn't believe that she had the power to do this, she just wasn't that high up. Then another thought came to him. She would push guards away, and have a new one. So had his services been dispensed with because she did get through quite a number of protectors.

What Finch was more concerned about was the coincidence of this and her position at the coffee shop. Did she in fact fit into a plan as the place had seemed to be a centre for activity lately? So apart from Pixel using her to get even with Sue, she could be part of something much bigger which was nothing to do with him whatsoever?

"I feel things are moving." Wren announced.

"No doubt," Finch answered "but in which direction?"

The family seemed normal. It was Monday evening and John was going to work soon. Denise was busy packing up his food box, and Sue was on her phone as usual. Kieran was upstairs.

"I don't know who you find to talk to all the time." Denise said as she passed Sue.

"I'm not talking to anyone in particular."

"What? Well that's not being very aware is it, I mean with all you hear these days?"

"It's social media Mam, get with it."

"Well that's even worse from what I hear."

Sue decided to turn the tables.

"So what sort of a day did you have then?"

"Oh you know regular boring stuff."

As they all shared each others knowledge Sue was tempted to ask if she felt better having had a funny turn but she wrapped it up a bit.

"Hope you're not overdoing it Mam, you've been looking a bit tired of late."

"Me? Oh I'm alright."

Then she went in for the kill.

"How's Gran?"

Denise stopped, knowing that her daughter would know of the day's events.

"Ok as far as I know. I'll give her a ring in a bit."

"We'll have to watch that she's not doing too much." The statement was loaded but didn't produce any visible response.

Denise was aware of what Sue was doing and concerned that she had actually raised the subject as it was an unwritten rule that you only spoke of things that concerned the outward show. There was definitely an undercurrent forming which could be picked up by any passing nosey spirit. John and Kieran also noted the ripple and tried to calm the area but somebody had picked up on it.

Hope had been waiting for this. It was a slight chink and that was all that was needed to start separating them into their own sectors and not work as a group. It was a dangerous tactic and should only be used by highly experienced operators and Sue hadn't been classed as that high. But all along the positions were changing. John would seem up one moment then down the next and Sue appeared to have more about her than it had appeared, so original suppositions were being questioned. Nobody was who they seemed to be and even their alter ego spirits were taking on a new appearance. The only one not involved appeared to be Kieran who didn't take part in any of their lifestyle apart from eating and sleeping at home.

Another player was also under scrutiny from Hope. Hannah. She hadn't seemed surprised at the sudden visit and for Dee to use a bodily image was strange. If they could communicate why not just do it like every other spirit. You didn't have to go and make such a song and dance of it. But that was probably what it was for.

Hope now was concerned. This sort of charade was used to cover other happenings so that nobody would give them any attention, but at this level what was the point? It couldn't have just been for the fun of it, but you didn't do that. If there was something Dee had to impart, to take such a risk was pointless. Couldn't she, as Denise just have rung her mother?

If Hannah had been a key player all along, surely Hope would have noticed so it must be that she was being used. An innocent party was often the brunt of some plot without realising it but it came back to the same question. "Why wasn't she surprised?"

This was something Wren and Finch were also chewing over.

Pixel couldn't just leave Lisa so that he could go in search of Sue. There were no willing stand-ins to help him out on this occasion, in fact most spirits were getting a bit tired of his irresponsible ways. It was one of those times when, if you put on a good act it became believable but to your cost. But he had to get to Sue, time was running out and he had to settle his score once and for all. As Lisa was being a bit of a pain, to put it mildly, he had got to use her now or she would kick off and that would be the end of it.

He saw her getting ready to go to her work and decided to stay in very close proximity for you never knew if a snippet might be picked up from the gran as to what Sue might be doing and when.

Fred took a box of plastic spoons to the coffee shop where Hannah was waiting for him.

"Those little wooden stirrers are best and they are cheaper." Hannah was surprised as the hospital always seemed to be making cuts.

Fred looked near the drinks area then turned back to her.

"There's no white sugar again." He liked a sweet cup of tea or coffee.

"Not good for you. Didn't you hear, it's brown now."

Fred waited for a gap in customers then walked over to her. "They have brown in coffee, white in tea. Always been like that."

She gave him a very hard stare

"Well things change. Like it or not."

"So no white.?"

"No white." She glared at him then returned to the till.

Fred may have seemed like the old plodder that went about his business but he didn't miss a trick. Someone was lifting it. He didn't voice this as Hannah's attitude had been a bit unusual and he wondered if she was the culprit. If it was only recently, maybe that young Lisa was pocketing a packet or two, or more, but Hannah would have had her head on a block for that. Stealing was not on, and meant instant dismissal, volunteer or no volunteer. Fred's mind then wandered to the small staff canteen and he decided that when it was convenient he would check there to see if there was any white, not just for his own use but to see if Hannah was being less than straightforward.

Hope had noticed his interest and it made her mull it over. She had always been in presence and hadn't noticed any such changes so what was going on?

Lisa had arrived on time and seemed keen to get on with her work for a change. There was a difference in her appearance which Hannah had spotted.

"Well, I'm pleased you took my advice about the heels. Those are much better. Not flat but they are more suitable."

"Wedges."

"Sorry, what was that?"

Lisa took a breath.

"They are called wedges, look." She lifted one leg to give the older woman a better view.

"Oh yes, well thank you for that. And may I say you are a much more attractive girl without all that muck plastered on your face."

While Lisa was getting a bit tired of the scrutiny, she didn't want to rub Hannah up the wrong way as she liked, no needed to be there for now. It was obvious she was making the woman nervous for at every opportunity she was scanning her up and down. In the end she knew she had to open her mouth.

"Look love, I'm making an effort ok? It may not be your style and I'm far from perfect but give me a chance, yeah?" She said but thought "And bloody well get off my back."

"Yes, yes, I can see that. Um, good." Hannah knew she had better give the girl a bit of space as there was something more than just a change of clothes going on here.

Fred had been pottering around a bit more than usual and Hannah was beginning to wonder why. In the end she waylaid him as he passed her till.

"You lost something Fred?"

"Lost? Me? What might I have lost then?"

He had an annoying little way of side stepping questions he didn't want to answer.

"Oh nothing."

She had a customer so her attention left him for a moment and when she looked back, he had gone, but not before he saw Lisa popping some packets of sugar into her pocket. He went about his business apparently oblivious to all around him but Fred didn't miss a trick.

Before she finished her shift, Lisa had pocketed as many small items as she could easily remove without being noticed. This new tabard was proving very useful because, with having two large pockets on the front the view was blocked to anyone behind her. Obviously she didn't take large things but flat packets like sugar, salt and pepper were perfect. And she hadn't seemed to bother too much when Fred had seen her, for she knew very well he had.

Pixel had been watching her and it even surprised him as she may have not been the best character to work with but he'd never known her to be a common thief. He wasn't covert in his thoughts, there was nothing sinister about his charge lifting things but that meant any passing lesser evil could pick up on it and use her on further occasions.

This is why people have often led a very clean life then suddenly start to steal or do other things they never would have dreamt of. It's often put down to mid life crisis, or being 'on the turn' and even senility with no proof of any of them.

But the fact is that exactly the same has happened to them as could very well be going to affect Lisa. The wayward spirit homes in on a human to either carry on where they left off when they were in body thus getting the satisfaction they were robbed of when they passed over, or take great delight in turning an upright citizen into a dishonest one or maybe a thug or even a murderer, depending on how they feel. Some go for the hardened criminals but others like the challenge of corruption.

So Lisa had almost lit a beacon and it would be a case of who got there first.

"Trust her." Pixel fumed. "Of all the stupid things to do." He might have known things were not going as planned, not with this one. Why did she have to draw attention to herself? He really was sick of her now and didn't care who knew it. Let some other guardian have her for a while.

It had quietened down a bit after the rush and Hannah was tidying up round the drinks dispenser. She looked at all the containers and smiled.

"So she fell for it! Now we've got her." She said under her breath but loud enough for anyone who wanted to listen.

Wren and Finch had been watching everyone and felt that things were building. People were communicating and not all that covertly. Yes they put on a façade for general viewing but they must have known that it wouldn't fool the trained spirit for a moment. So what was the game? They were hovering over the coffee shop to see if they could pick up any traces of any other visitors that were unusual in any way. Suddenly Finch indicated to one of the trays at the dispenser section. A packet of sugar had been opened and then put back as if someone had realised it was brown and didn't want it.

"Not unusual." Wren wasn't that impressed.

Finch was examining it closely then suddenly pulled back.

"It's in the sugar!"

"What is?" But as soon as he'd asked the question Wren knew. "The dust, the brown dust, you wouldn't see it and it's in packets."

"Which means it's been here a while because it has had to have been deposited at the packaging plant before the stuff ended up in these."

"Or before." Wren was going right back. "What if it was there when the beets were growing?"

"We'll have to check that, but for now we have to find out just how much sugar has been affected because that is spreading the evil remains back on earth."

Wren also had a thought. "If it's hidden in the brown sugar, where else?" His attention turned to the salt and pepper packets. As the salt was white it seemed unlikely to be there, but they would still have to check.

"Hang on, I don't think so." Finch remembered something. "You remember Fred asked abut the white sugar and was told there wasn't any. So what would that do?"

Wren said "They'd either have to have sweeteners or…brown."

"Yes, forcing them to turn to the brown. So I don't think it is in the white salt, just the brown pepper."

"And what else?" Wren continued thinking." Any brown powder that is consumed, and that's how the evil will take over the minds and bodies and build up an army almost."

"We've got to move. We don't know how long this has been going on as we've agreed."

"And how long before the effects start to manifest?" Wren was still churning it over.

"That's something we can't know because it could be a long term placing waiting for a trigger, or it could be a lesser evil just wanting to stir things up a bit, that's happened before as we know only too well."

"Haven't got many answers have we?"

Finch was silent for a moment then said. "No but we do have a lead."

"Of course we do. Lisa."

"She must be monitored constantly, but not by us. Don't want her suspecting. Just want her to act in whatever way they have planned."

Wren felt this was using her as a guinea pig but there was no other way. They had to find out in what way the evil was going to manipulate her, and also how many more souls were already under their power.

"Wait a minute." Wren had a sudden thought.

"Go on?" Finch didn't want any more time to lapse but had to listen.

"What if the coffee shop is a hub?"

There was a pause before Finch answered. He was recapping on recent happenings.

"You could have something. We think Hannah summoned Denise, as Dee to go there and something must have been exchanged or they wouldn't have met in person, too dangerous, and Dee changed her appearance. But we aren't sure if Hope was manipulating it and sent out a false message to get her there because on appearances the two didn't communicate spiritually did they?"

"It was a weird one. And Dee seemed in control when she got back and she was gunning for someone." Wren had been eavesdropping and remembered it.

Finch brought it back to Wren's suggestion.

“So after Dee had been, there is no white sugar and we know the brown contains brown dust. And possibly the pepper too.”

“Someone is spreading the evil.” Wren sounded positive. “And using the coffee place as a deposit and collection point.”

“And those involved know it, so none of them are there by chance. I think even Lisa is there as a placement.” Finch seemed certain as it all fell into place.

“You mean knowingly?” Wren queried. “Don’t think so. She’s hardly the brightest button in the box.”

“But they don’t have to be. They get promised wonderful things. You do this for me, and…well you know the rest.”

“But who would be using her, I mean directing her?”

Finch was ready to move. “That, my friend is just what we intend to find out.”

“Well we’d better move. I don’t like the way this is going.” Wren almost sulked.

His partner gave him the impression of raised eyebrows and a little shake of the head, spiritually of course.

Chapter 12

The high level angels had scouts watching Mars and the moon constantly and even the slightest movement was monitored and recorded. But it didn't end there. From experience they knew that they had to take a wider view because the main threat wasn't always where the action was. Decoy positions were a common thing but thanks to man's increasing knowledge, the evil had new tools to play with. With nearly five thousand satellites orbiting the earth, it was like a playground. If they got tired of using one, they just transferred to another. Rocket bodies were a common vehicle but it had taken a while before it was noticed that they were a 'departure lounge' waiting to deposit evil cells in just the right locations.

A massive sweep had cleared most but as soon as it had been completed another group would appear. In fact anything that mankind had sent into space was a target for waiting evil to attack. The suggestion that certain space experiments were jinxed held more truth than anyone would expect or be able to prove.

Of course this wasn't being ignored, the good were constantly fighting and on some occasions it was only due to their intervention that further possible disasters were thwarted. That in turn made the evil angry and so they would then retaliate and so the fight goes on. Space is not a placid area spiritually.

Sue was aware she had to find a way to rid herself of anyone who was likely to hinder her. She had an objective and the likes of Pixel were a definite threat so she had to think fast, but for the plan to succeed, she had to somehow break her thought ties with the family which wasn't going to be easy. There was a way of blocking but that would not only make the rest of the group suspicious but any onlookers, and there were plenty of those. This called for an unusual tactic.

You really think you are going to be privy to that? You haven't been paying attention.

Let us just say, without going into the transition process, that she could vaporise into the air, not her body, her spirit. She could then merge with the atmosphere, breaking up and rejoining so it was difficult to keep track of her. The family would still think they were in communication so not suspect, that was the trick.

Let's put it in fairly simple terms for those who must have an explanation.

You are in a room and you hear someone talking in the next room so you know they are there, right? Wrong. It can be a recording, been used in films, television programmes. You believe what you are meant to believe, not what is actual fact.

So if Sue leaves the impression of her spirit still being in situ, it will be accepted and don't forget the first rule. You do not ask questions of a fellow member.

She was now free to move anywhere and even the likes of Wren and Finch wouldn't be able to detect her. Her first call was to Pixel who was hovering around Lisa because he had to, and was still planning to leave as soon as he had finished with her. She hadn't done a very good job of getting him close to Sue. It wasn't much to ask, but beyond her boundaries it seemed. To say he considered her a useless piece of flotsam is the polite way of putting what he felt. It was obvious he had a fixation on what had gone on in the past but to Sue it was just that. Past, gone, end of. She was going to try a therapy which may or may not work but it was worth a try and she knew it would be dangerous. She had to reprogram his spirit.

If this sounds very personal, it is far from it for the results could have an effect on a lot that was going on elsewhere, for while he was being tunnel visioned he wasn't concentrating on other work he should be doing, so it was up to her to break the tie.

Although he had felt he could just use Lisa to get to his intended, that was nothing to do with his current purpose, and the powers that be were insisting he get his spiritual digit out and get to work.

She was now watching Lisa, sprawled out in her usual ungainly fashion while Pixel was just floating around appearing totally bored. Sue called on a stand in to protect Lisa for that would be essential but would also trigger Pixel into action.

"What the…." He jumped.

"You wanted a break. Now you've got one." The thought was in his mind but he wasn't aware of anyone there.

"What are you doing here?" His tone changed thinking he had been sent a replacement.

There was no reply. The stand in just observed him and hovered near Lisa.

"Then they've replaced me. My prayers have been answered. Right. She's all yours. I'm off."

Nothing happened. He tried to just float off into the atmosphere but he was still in the room. This made him angry and he started flinging himself around like a caged animal.

Suddenly he felt a pressure, not in one place, all over and he was tumbling and becoming disorientated. He tried to ask what was happening but he seemed to have lost all control.

Now Sue had him in the right state, she set to work clearing some of his memories and replacing them with similar but slightly different versions of what had actually gone on. No longer did he have an issue with her, in fact he would barely know her and from now on and would only think of her as someone who he had briefly encountered way back. He had been hindering her but now she was free to complete the job she was supposed to be doing.

Although the brief explanation sounds simple, it takes many centuries of perfecting to make sure it works effectively and cannot be used by anyone who just thinks it would be a good idea. There are only so many who make the grade to be able to practice it.

Lisa would put down any change in his ways to him being a pain in the rear and not knowing where he was going, except for annoying people. In fact she was beginning to feel it was time to oust him and ask for another guardian, not that she felt she needed one but it was one of those things she knew was compulsory.

The job completed Sue resumed her normal position with no one being any the wiser.

Wren and Finch were at the coffee shop long before it opened on Tuesday morning. They had checked all the packages and everything seemed to be as it was the day before. One thing that concerned them was the fact that, if the bags contained Mars dust, why hadn't the higher levels done something to remove them? The same question came up continually.

"Anyone who takes any of it into their body will be affected by the evil." Wren was still hovering over the drinks area.

"I don't like it." Finch seemed edgy. "Why are they leaving it? Something must be done before it's too late."

"Well we can't so it will have to stay where it is." Wren concluded.

Suddenly a noise took them unawares

"It's only the old fool." Finch fobbed it off.

Fred was getting ready to unlock the shutter as soon as Hannah arrived.

"Hm, wonder who we'll have today." He said to himself. He moved along slightly then back which made the two spirits nervous.

"Does he know we're here?" Wren imparted.

"How can he?" Finch was about to ignore it when he stopped and said "Shouldn't go on appearances. Let's have a look."

Instantly they were on either side of him and he stopped and stood perfectly still.

If anyone from the spirit side was watching it could have looked quite funny, all three in a row completely still.

"Morning Fred."

The voice broke the moment and Fred was now alone.

"Oh hello Hannah, let's get you inside." And he pressed the button to raise the shutters. He usually left her to it but something he had just felt made him follow her in. He went round the shop and gave a satisfied nod as he walked out.

"You lost something Fred?" Hannah was curious.

"No, no, it's ok, just checking the floor love. Some of them can spill stuff and its best to know now before they all come trampling in."

"Oh you are thoughtful Fred, wish there were more like you."

Little did she realise that he had experienced at least one presence a few seconds earlier and wanted to check the air was clear.

She knew very well the 'new' lady wouldn't be back, there was no need now. Lisa had been asked to come in earlier so at least there would be someone to help.

"Well we'll see what today brings." She said to herself.

"More than you think." Wren couldn't help adding.

"If the packets contain what we think." Finch agreed.

Denise had gone to work as usual but had done something rather strange. She had taken a flask of coffee with her instead of using the dispenser in the office block. This didn't go unnoticed by anyone.

"Why you doing that?" John had asked before he went to bed as he was back on nights.

"Oh I'm getting particular." She laughed. "Anyway I'm not sure how clean those things are and I've gone off the taste anyway."

But Wren and Finch put a totally different meaning on it. They knew she must have done something after her visit to the hospital the day before. But that didn't add up. There were so many buttons to press on these vending machines that if you wanted coffee or tea with sugar you pressed different ones to those without. And unless you restocked the machines from inside, there was no way any of the contents could be tampered with. But it was still too much of a coincidence to ignore so they made a point of keeping a close eye on her that day.

Kieran was reluctantly getting ready for the academy as it was exam time and he felt tired from revising.

"Do you know what you are going to do yet?" His mum asked almost absent mindedly.

There was a big sigh.

"It hasn't changed mum. Still the same."

"Well I think you should have other options. If you don't get to do what you want you should have something to fall back on. Don't you agree John?"

"Eh?" He was looking at the morning paper which had just arrived.

"I was saying, about our Kieran, he should have something else."

"Oh yes." He answered not having a clue what she was on about but it sounded about right.

"Now Sue has her heart set on doing something in space." Denise was still busying about in the kitchen.

There was no reply so she carried on getting ready.

"Right, there's some ham in the fridge for lunch when you get up, you can make yourself a sandwich, but you'll need to take some bread out." She was moving about as quickly as she was talking but John got the gist of it.

Within a short time the three had left and John was alone. He didn't feel like going straight to bed. Sometimes he just liked to settle a bit, have a cup of tea and then get his head down. But today something was making him sleep now, for a communication had to be made.

Finch was hovering over the house for he had a gut feeling, if spirits have guts that is, that something was imminent. He had left Wren watching the coffee shop for he was still convinced it could be a hub for receiving and despatching.

Something was happening. There was a bright cloud surrounding John as his spirit side Jay rose up. There were other spirits there but it was so bright it was difficult for Finch to work out how many, but he wasn't prepared for the next thing. They all turned and Jay started to increase in size as he pointed to Finch. The light wasn't bright now but an eerie greeny blue verging on black and the feeling was of pure evil.

Finch didn't hang around to find out any more but was immediately back with Wren and showing signs of terror throughout his entire being.

"What has happened to you?" Wren was staggered.

It took Finch a few moments to calm himself and he pulled his friend away from the shop to a quieter place for a moment.

"It's him!"

"Who is him?" Wren was puzzled.

"Her husband. He is evil, and for all we know they all are."

Wren calmed him down and demanded a full account of what had happened.

"So he didn't make contact with you?"

"I-I-don't think so, it's hard to tell."

Wren thought for a moment and then said "Well they obviously knew you were there and didn't want you around."

“Yes. I’d gathered that much.” Finch sounded sarcastic which was how he felt. He sometimes wished his partner didn’t just state the obvious.

“Are you going back?”

The silence and unseen feeling said it all. After a moment Wren ventured another useless comment.

“So it’s John then.” He didn’t really know what else to offer and wished Finch could have been more specific.

As the coffee shop was fairly quiet they decided to retreat and way things up after this new occurrence.

Stop for a moment. With all the concentration on one area, it is easy to get drawn into the fact that this is the only thing that is going on and that everywhere else life is sailing along smoothly. But the happenings and placements in this area are all over the globe with more concentration in highly populated areas. That isn’t to say the barren parts are ignored, far from it. From the very depths of the oceans, across the deserts and up to the highest mountains, every inch in covered in some way. And this is just Earth. Expand that to our solar system, the Milky Way and beyond, in fact the whole universe for as much as we know of it.

Now imagine the fight between good and evil on that scale then come back to the area we are concentrating on. Puts it in perspective a bit doesn’t it?

The watchers noticed the usual deposits arriving on Mars but apart from that nothing appeared to be disturbing the dust. The amounts coming in could vary according to how much evil was being destroyed but there was never a time when it was not being used. Maybe it was the extreme cover by the good forces that had halted the attention of their enemies but in some ways it was too normal. We aren’t going to say that they keep account books for how much is received and in turn how much was removed, but in the spirit world they just know. So if any amount to the smallest grain had been moved, it would have been noted. This could have put a question over the brown dust appearing in sugar at the coffee shop, but the high angels already had the answer to that. There was no need to explain it to Wren and Finch at this stage as they wanted them to stay alert and not miss a trick.

Lisa arrived at the shop but looked decidedly bored.

"We could get busy later." Hannah told her. "One of the rooms is being used for a conference."

"Well they won't come here, not if they're a posh lot." Lisa slowly put on her tabard.

"No but what happens is that we send food and drinks in to them."

Lisa stopped and looked at her.

"What, in the packets and in cardboard mugs?"

Hannah sighed. There was a lot this girl had to learn.

"If you're interested," she paused to make sure Lisa was paying attention, "we get it altogether, then one of the staff comes and takes it then they put the food on plates and the coffee in cups."

"To make it look posh."

"Well, more presentable."

"What a load of faff."

Hannah had to admit that while this exchange was going on Lisa was busying about, even fussing over whether the paper napkins were straight.

"I'll make something of her yet." She thought.

"Oh look." Lisa was at the drinks machine. "We've got white sugar again. Ha, shows you how important it was to be healthy doesn't it?"

"Oh?" Hannah was surprised she hadn't noticed it but she had gone straight to the serving area so she must have missed it but she'd make a point of asking Fred what he knew about it next time he passed.

Wren and Finch, not wanting to be away too long had picked up on this as they returned. Immediately they hovered over the brown sugar packets. They didn't need to be open for them to notice that they contained nothing but sugar.

"So where did the dust go?" Wren was the first to wonder.

If Finch could have sighed again he would.

“Isn’t it obvious? Only certain ones were infected and they have been taken, and possibly consumed.”

“So the evil is already out there?”

“It must be.” Finch was still churning it over. “Think how many people have been through here and where they could be now? They could have gone home, to work, or even on holiday.”

“So it could be anywhere.”

“Or everywhere.” Finch added.

After a minute Wren said, “That Denise took some, Lisa took some that we know of and they didn’t just take one.”

They were silent for a while as they didn’t seem to be coming up with any answers. Things weren’t falling into place.

“I think we’re looking in the wrong location.” Finch decided

“Explain.”

“We are concentrating on this coffee shop which we think could be a hub but shouldn’t we be looking more to where the stuff has gone to rather than here? We know it was here.”

Wren wanted to come up with a solution himself.

“I know. One of us go to Dee, well Denise’s place and check on them there and the other check on Lisa’s place. There must be traces of it at one or both.”

Finch had to admit, as flimsy as it was, they couldn’t overlook it as not being important.

“Which do you want?” He asked.

“I don’t mind.”

This sort of reply always niggled Finch who preferred straight answers.

“Right. That’s settled then.” He stated. “We check out both together.”

Wren wasn’t entirely sure that he had got his own way after all, as that wasn’t exactly what he had suggested.

Sue was feeling free and very relieved that she had performed the treatment successfully. Now without Pixel hanging on to her, she could do the job she came to do and the sooner the better although she knew you couldn’t rush these things. It also meant that Lisa should also back off but she seemed to be a lonely soul inside and before long she would have to reach out to somebody.

“Ha, I’d have to reach out too if he was my guardian.” She laughed as she arrived at work.

“You been on a date?” One of her fellow workers asked.

“No. Just cleared some junk out of my life.” She laughed.

“Ooo, what’s his name?

“Who said it was a ‘he’?

“Oh nothing, it’s just that I could do with a change if you know what I mean, and if he’s going spare….”

“Forget it. Nothing like that.”

“Oh. Disappointing.”

Today she was restocking some of the shelves which was lucky as it gave her a chance to keep a watchful eye not only the products but the shelving itself. She was very well aware of the continual alert for dust of any colour as long as it wasn’t what you would expect to find in any one place. There was rarely any normal dust as the stock was rotated and the units dusted on a regular basis which meant that anything untoward would stand out.

For most of the morning everything had gone alright, almost to the point of being a bit boring but she had to remind herself that this was what she was here for and to miss the slightest thing could have ongoing disastrous effects. It was nearing lunch time and she was just going to reload one shelf when her hand rubbed against something sharp. Without thinking she cried out and another worker asked her what was the matter.

“I-I- don’t know, I seem to have cut myself. There was something sticking out but I can’t see it now.”

Her hand was bleeding and someone fetched the manager who sent her to the first aid room immediately. He also allocated the other worker to clear the floor for safety but also to see what it was that had caused this.

“There’s nothing,” she said, “the whole shelf is smooth and if something was there she must have knocked it somewhere.”

But there had been a sharp object, and it wouldn’t be found. Sue kept her thoughts inside but the rest of the group knew that the enemy was coming out of the woodwork. This was just what they had hoped would happen soon and it was possible that Sue had come a bit too near. Straight away other spirits were sent in to examine the area but could only report that something had been in presence and left, although there was a faint wake.

The family knew that it didn't have to be the physical area that had stirred up something, but the fact that one or all of them were getting too close so now the evil would use any means to stop them. This was just a warning to back off. Next time it could be fatal and although that wouldn't stop the spiritual side if could halt or delay any plans the rest of the group had for running their quarry to ground.

The other family members were on extra guard but it had to be covert. Each knew they could be the next target, for instead of attacking them as a family they would probably pick them off one by one, thus creating confusion and plans having to be changed constantly.

Kieran was very aware although to look at him nobody would have given him a second glance. He was a typical teenager, had to do his studies at the academy, spent time on his computer, didn't mix much and wasn't particular polite to his parents and of course didn't see why he should tidy his room. His teachers always felt he had a lot more to offer but hoped it would manifest as he got older.

He was walking back to class when a fight started in front of him.

"Oh not them again." He thought.

It was the two same boys who always seemed to be having a go at each other. Most of the others lads walked by having a laugh and cheering on one or the other. When the inevitable happened and a teacher arrived on the scene it was the precise moment when one of the boys' legs came out and tripped Kieran over so there were three of them on the floor.

Anyone who has been wrongly accused will know the feeling exactly. You've done nothing, got dragged into something then blamed. At the end of it the teacher would probably accuse him of starting it.

But they weren't dealing with an everyday student and although it was against the rules, Kane rose and urged some of the boys to speak. They would never know why they did it.

"But sir, he wasn't in it."

"No he got kicked sir. We saw it."

But it wasn't going to work.

"And who asked you for your opinion?"

They began to wonder why they had put themselves in the firing line.

"Right all of you report to my office after this lesson."

"But sir…."

The look froze the boy to the ground.

It wasn't the fact that he had got to report and would no doubt be punished, but Kieran had fallen in such a way his knee was very painful resulting in a distinct limp. If it didn't improve he would insist on being seen by the resident nurse.

The big question was 'who's next?' Something was definitely moving and was going to jeopardise the group.

Wren and Finch had homed in on these events but it raised the question, if they weren't working together, why take them out one at a time. Could it be that the evil guessed all their plans and were making several tasks into one?

It must mean they were a high risk for such desperate steps to be taken and how much of a threat for no one knew what any of their objectives were. But something was coming to a head and it seemed imminent.

Time for a bit of strategy. One of them could watch Denise while the other took John. Simple except for one fact. Nothing would get past Finch but Wren could easily miss something and both people needed equal protection. So they resorted to another little trick. Finch would monitor Denise as she seemed to be a more active player and while Wren was covering John, everything would also be relayed to his partner. This tool was used when young spirits were in training. Their mentor would sent them out on a task but would attach, for the want of a better word, a bug so they could observe everything they encountered and be ready to jump in if necessary.

As time was important they went straight into position but neither of them were ready for what they were about to encounter.

Chapter 13

It was getting toward the end of the shift and before Hannah could even suggest it, Lisa had started to check round the shop, picking up bits of paper and wiping down the surfaces.

"Do you think you might stay here for a while then?" She asked.

Lisa didn't look up but said "I might."

"Trouble is I suppose you need a paid job." Hannah was fishing.

"Well yeah, but if I can prove I'm looking and not staying idle, they'll keep paying my benefit."

"Oh." Hannah was confused. "I don't quite get this modern way of doing things. When I was young we had to go to work and bring the money into the home."

"Bit different now."

Hannah still wasn't giving up.

"Well you need something, I mean you can't just keep doing voluntary work."

Lisa looked at her now.

"Well, we don't always know why we do things do we?"

There was silence. Hannah thought that was a strange answer even for Lisa. But it wasn't picked up as the two regular sentinels were elsewhere.

"Oh Fred." Hannah called as he passed but paused and came over to her.

"What's up?"

"Oh nothing, it's just that there is some white sugar now."

"Oh yes, I enjoyed my drink better today. Saw it when we opened."

"But you didn't say." Hannah felt put out.

"I'm not with you." He looked bewildered. Surely she would have known before he did as she must have filled the containers.

"Fred," Hannah was very thoughtful "I didn't know it was there. I didn't put it out."

"Blow me." He too was now pondering. "Well, I'll tell you what I think."

"Please do, I'd like some sort of explanation to it all."

"They must have done it while we were off. They have keys and they could easily have come in and put the sugar there."

Hannah laughed.

"And when, tell me, have you ever known them to lift a finger for anything?"

"Ah you got me there." He used the answer to make a quick exit as this was getting to intense and he knew Hannah wasn't satisfied and wanted answers.

The truth was that he had put the white sugar out having removed it in the first place. He had also put the contaminated brown sugar there and had now removed that. But neither Hannah nor anyone else must know about it. He relied on the fact that any complaints to the management may be looked at but they had more important issues than the colour of sugar. And if Hannah kept on they would put it down to a senior moment, especially when the sugar was now as it should be.

Fred knew that Lisa had taken all this in her stride so the only person now concerned seemed to be Hannah and she had to be careful or it may be suggested she was getting too old for the job.

John was asleep lying on top of the bed. Wren hovered at a safe distance aware that Jay would pick up his presence but up to now everything seemed alright. Then he noticed Jay wasn't in the area and so he ventured a bit closer. Everything looked in order but then a thought hit him. What if it wasn't the physical they were after and the other two incidents were merely to throw anyone off the scent. The evil were actually after their spirits and what happened to the bodies was just an initial warning of what could follow, for if the body was terminated they would have the free sprits in their control.

The other fact was that none of the four had additional guardians so they could not step in. Jay was John so what happened to one should affect the other. But if say John was killed, Jay would carry on in spirit the same as any other person. This was getting a bit confusing for Wren but he remembered that Finch was monitoring everything so when they next met he would get his answers.

The problem was that Wren's 'bug' had been deactivated, but he was unaware of it.

Meanwhile Finch was hovering around Denise who was busy at her computer. In a similar situation to John, Dee was there but she wasn't alone. Finch became aware of another presence behind him and it wasn't good. In body he would have felt the icy fingers running down his back which wasn't altogether different to the feeling he was getting in spirit.

"You think you are so good. Know it all. One step ahead." The thoughts were being put into his being.

"Who are you?" He demanded.

The answer came as a bit of a shock.

"Where are you?"

This was a strange thing to ask. Wasn't it obvious? Unless of course this was a lowly playful sprite have a bit of fun with him.

"Alright you've had your fun now go!"

"Oh I'm not playing my friend."

"Don't call me your friend. I am not your friend."

There was a pause and Finch could have thought he was alone but he could feel the presence closing in on him.

"May I point out one small detail?" The message was loaded with sarcasm but Finch obviously needed to know.

"Go on, if it keeps you happy." The reply was equally ironical.

"You two little lads are pre empting the next incident, so you are covering the two most likely candidates."

"Have you anything to say that isn't obvious?" He was getting very impatient. He needed whoever it was to come to the point and stop dancing around it.

Again the same question.

"Where are you?" The tone was very sinister now.

"That's it I've had enough of your childish pranks, now I suggest you clear off and go and worry some other unsuspecting soul."

"Well you obviously aren't getting it."

Before Finch could come out with any more remarks to be ignored the visitor continued.

"You could have fallen straight into the trap."

Finch was silent now.

"You have two minor incidents and you rush straight off to spy on someone else."

"Are you trying to suggest that we are cowards?" He was fuming now.

"Not at all. A bit thick maybe."

He knew this would raise Finch's hackles to the limit so without waiting for an answer he carried on. "Didn't you even think for a moment that it was what was planned, to get you out of the way so that a second strike could be made, a fatal one?"

Now he had Finch's attention. Of course, they had up and left thinking they had to watch the parents, but if that was a plot they had rushed headlong into it.

"Not what one would expect from highly trained operatives wouldn't you say?"

The words hung in the air as the presence left but the fact was, they were true. That was exactly what they had done and what was worse, how many had witnessed it. They would be a laughing stock. There was only one answer, they must stop the next hit at all costs in order to redeem themselves.

A new piece of information was now rocking the boat. There was a rumour going around that the family were thinking of moving. This could mean that they had to get away from the surrounding area physically for some reason, and spiritually because there was far too much attention on them which was the last thing they wanted. This was a common problem when sentinels often hindered rather than helped. And what would happen to Hannah?

But it could also mean that the job or jobs they had been allocated were finished. But that would mean that all four were complete or they couldn't leave. Also, they could have fooled the watchers into thinking they worked alone but were in fact the combined cell that was first thought.

As word spreads quickly, and even in an instant in the spirit world, it was no longer a secret.

Wren and Finch were debating as to whether they should pull back now because with the current attention of the group they didn't want to look inefficient again. At their level they were still answerable to the higher levels, but they were nowhere near the top, wherever that was for no one was sure.

When the inevitable request from above came, it was no surprise but how were the two going to explain their actions? Also it could hamper their climb further up the ladder.

In earthly terms, when you are waiting for news, or an appointment you don't want to keep, the time seems to drag, but if you are enjoying yourself the time seems to fly. That is a very simple version of what happens in the spiritual sector. There it can be manipulated to suit the needs, so in this case Wren and Finch would know they had to attend a scrutiny, but wouldn't know when. They would be called at a moment's notice and that would mean literally that moment without delay. But of course the summons could be hung out for as long as the hierarchy wished and waiting is the worst thing for putting even spirits on edge and also makes them very vulnerable because they are not in charge.

So what could they do during this period? Carry on as though nothing had happened or just hover around doing nothing. Finch came up with an idea.

"If we have the time, maybe we could get more information."

"You'll have to explain that." Wren wasn't keen on putting his proverbial foot in it any more than necessary.

"Well, just supposing we could stop the next attack, or warning, wouldn't that redeem us at least a bit?"

"It might, but what precisely did you have in mind? I hope it won't land us further…"

"Look," Finch was getting edgy knowing it would take a lot of explaining to the high levels "we can't just hang around, we've got to do something to get us off the hook. And you haven't realised that this is precisely what they could be doing, seeing if we do take the initiative, hence the wait."

Wren had been in Finch's shadow all along and had accepted everything he said or planned without question, but now he started to think for himself and wasn't at all happy at this latest suggestion. Personally, he would rather face the music and get it over and done with, whatever the outcome as he wasn't the ambitious level climber that his partner was.

Finch just wanted to get as high as he could and then start ruling those beneath him and he was only too well aware that this latest episode could have ruined all his chances, thanks to pairing him with such a useless article. One would have thought that it was perfect because Wren had gone along with him, whereas someone with a bit of 'go' in them wouldn't have co-operated at all and then where would he have been?

The part of the earth where the family lived was now in darkness. There was a strange stillness in the area as though everyone was waiting. The call came, the two had been summoned

They were instantly in the area where they had been communicating with their higher levels and were surprised at the pleasant atmosphere that surrounded them but this was a bit different. Usually there were two or three high spirits in presence but now they seemed to be surrounded but they couldn't actually see them, in spiritual terms of course, but they heard a familiar voice.

Please remember that spirits communicate in thought but to make it easier to understand this is written as the spoken word.

"So you have been very busy?" That was the one they usually interacted with which put them at ease slightly, which was the intention.

"Well we hope so. "Finch was bound to be the one to answer.

"And how near are you now to resolving this?"

It was going better than they thought, they might just be lucky.

"Well…" Finch started but was quickly interrupted.

"You are no further forward now than you were at the beginning."

The tone was very harsh and accusing and the whole atmosphere was changing. They could feel the unseen spirits closing in on them.

"Oh but we are…" Finch was again cut off.

"Well your little plan didn't work. Maybe next time they will send people with more experience."

This wasn't what they wanted to hear and dreaded what was coming next. The chief spirit now seemed to be growing until Wren and Finch felt tiny in comparison and they had good cause to be nervous. Finch tried one last desperate attempt to wriggle out of it.

"Look we only did what we were told, we didn't really want to…."

"Enough. Don't take us for fools, we knew from the start."

It was Wren's turn, not as the simpering underling but his own being came to the fore.

"Well, what you think you knew was wrong. You are the ones who have messed up this operation and you will have to answer to a much higher force now. You have totally smashed the chance to expose the evil we had in our sights."

There was a hush for a moment before the chief continued.

"Fighting to the bitter end. It will do you no good."

Before either could retaliate the chief came in with his final blow. The ensemble was growing and the two felt trapped.

"You felt extremely clever because you had so easily infiltrated our area but you only did so because we allowed you in to monitor you and find out what we needed to know."

The entire area was now deathly still.

He continued.

"Did you really think two evil elements like yourselves could get into our realms just like that? And what have you learned? Nothing. The Mars dust is common knowledge but one thing you didn't think we had noticed was that you knew who the dispatchers and receivers were. There was no need for a herald, you managed the job without help."

There was nothing the two could say, not that they would have been given the chance.

"And of course we gave you plenty to investigate while we were monitoring your evil activities."

He waited for that to sink in and said "Any questions?"

Wren was first.

"You aren't referring to the cell, the family who are not what they seem to be?"

There was humour in the reply.

"You see while you were so busy chasing false situations, you failed to notice how much you were being examined, and it was very enlightening."

"The four are special operatives aren't they, decoys you placed?" Wren almost spat out.

There was another pause for the answer to hit home.

"Oh they all were."

The eerie stillness was growing.

"Not everyone? Not the old lady, and the tart and…" Finch ventured now.

"Every single one of them and didn't they play brilliant parts?" The reply was loaded with sarcasm.

"But, the brown dust?"

"Props. We rather liked that one. For your satisfaction, Fred removed the white and placed the contaminated brown, then removed it and put the white back. But it was harmless and wouldn't have hurt even a microbe. We had had to let you think you had messed up big time before you could send any further messages back."

The stillness continued before the final blow. The tone of the spirit was changing, he was now not only the judge but the executioner.

"We let you think you had entered our realms to spy, but in fact we were the spies and what we found was ultimate evil at work. Your job was to select specific locations and have the evil returned to the planet where it could spread and eventually take over even though it meant the destruction of Earth. Your connection to Mars has been destroyed, as have any deposits you transferred here. For every move you made, we counteracted it. The planet is now clean and we intend to keep it that way."

The two were still turning things over wondering how they had walked into the trap so easily but they were dealing with high powers who had them exactly where they wanted them at any time.

Everything was very still and Finch was forced to ask.

"So, you will be sending us back?"

The pause seemed to go on for ever but then the final blow came.

"You are not that stupid that you don't know what happens to ultimate evil, whether they be servants or the organisers."

Both Wren and Finch were now regretting the question and the answer came straight away.

“Evil of this kind has one destination, a magenta hole.”

“But you have no right…” Wren tried in desperation for leniency.

“And you have no say. You would willingly have destroyed this earth and more with no qualms or conscience so you face the penalty. And may I add, any others who think they can achieve it.”

Finch started to laugh.

“Oh dear. You don’t know everything even if you think you do.”

This was met with silence forcing him to continue.

“You really think you can take us to the event horizon and shove us in the hole?” He laughed again with more confidence this time. “Well let me tell you something my friend. You are aware that even you don’t know the exact position of it so we won’t let go of whoever is holding us, and when we go, they go. Bye bye guards.” His laughter was that of a madman.

This time the silence was uncanny and there seemed to be a very slight movement in the atmosphere as the archangel delivered the final blow.

“Oh we don’t escort you to the magenta hole. You didn’t know that? Common mistake. We have given your positions. The hole will get you. And by the way, you haven’t realised that the nearest one is right next to Mars. Obvious really. When the souls are despatched the earth dust is deposited at the same time.”

It barely had time to sink in before a whoosh took them both, stretching their evil souls like strips of spun sugar. The remaining area was now still in a different way.

“Just one last job to do.”

They all gathered round in concentration.

“In case one of you players happened to be a member of The Team, thank you.”

For although it could not be confirmed, it was suspected that someone who kept their head down had contributed to the success of this operation.

Final Warning.

Do not disturb the dust on Mars or sure as anything

THE HOLE WILL GET YOU

About the Author

Tabbie Browne grew up in the Cotswolds in central England which is where she gets the inspiration for her novels. Her father had very strong spiritual beliefs and she feels he guides her but always with a warning to stay in control of your own mind.

Her earliest recollection of writing was at primary school and it has seemed to play a part at significant times during her life. She thinks it is only when we are forced to take step back and unclutter our minds for a while we realise our potential. This point was proved when she slipped a disc, and being very immobile had to write in pencil as the ink would not flow upwards! At this time she wrote many comical poems which, when able again, performed to many audiences. Comedy is very difficult but you know if you are a success with a live audience.

In 1991 as a collector of novelty salt and pepper shakers, she realised there was no book in the UK devoted entirely to the subject. So she wrote one. Which meant she achieved the fact that it was the first of its kind in the country and it sold well to like collectors not only in the UK but in the USA.

Another large upheaval came when she was diagnosed with breast cancer, and due to the extreme energy draining, found it difficult to work for an employer. So she took a freelance journalist course and was pleased to have articles accepted, her main joy being the piece about her father and his life in the village. Again the inspiration area.

But the novels were eating away inside and drawing on her experience at stamp and coin fairs she wrote *'A Fair Collection'* which she serialised in the magazine 'Squirrels' for people who hoard things.

When she wrote *'White Noise Is Heavenly Blue'* and its sequel *'The Spiral'* she sat at the keyboard and the titles just came to her, as did the content of the books. There is no way she could write the plot first as she never knew what was coming next, almost as if somebody was dictating, and for that reason she could never change anything.

Loves:
Animals,
Also performing in live theatre and working as a tv supporting artiste.

Hates:
Bad manners,
Insincere people.